Hearts of Monsters

For Christina

Jeremy Megargee

HEARTS OF MONSTERS FIRST EDITION

ISBN-9781797674278

www.facebook.com/JMHorrorFiction

Cover design by Mitch Green @ RadPressPublishing

This book is inspired by the writing styles of Charles Bukowski and Cormac McCarthy. Minimal capitalization and punctuation, just the raw meat of the story presented from flawed and monstrous perspectives...

"There is no exquisite beauty without some strangeness in the proportion."

- Edgar Allan Poe

Witch

the snakes copulate in pits, writhing madness it's for me they slither, just a show for a crone, breeding in return for the bleeding.

i'm a crone only in the sense of mental maturation, for the glamour of youth still holds sway over me.

borrowed youth, or maybe you'd call it stolen, but a pretty face is mine to wield in times of necessity. the new age, witchcraft to wicca, the old ways falling to the new trends. i am a remnant of the trials, the burning times, Salem's sins, sins of fathers, mothers, daughters, and sons…

villages became towns. towns became cities. cities of nesting insects, polluted fog, an overpopulation of flesh and blood producing more flesh and blood. i watch alone, roof of straw, floor of mud, walls timber from long dead trees.

how long can it last? this world they've made? this world they've profaned and defiled. the soil weeps. the trees droop. the sky becomes a bruise, and soon the rain will drip down red. it's abuse. it's cruel, thoughtless abuse.

don't they see?

why can't they see?

Wolf

i am violence. it's trapped inside, teeth, claws, and all the primitive instincts that belong to the wolf. i am man, i am wolf, i am both. unnatural symmetry. a schism i've learned to live with.

it takes time to come to terms with the shift, the hunger, and the lunar phases of the moon. they say that you can get used to just about anything as long as it becomes routine, something habitual. the beast in me is habitual. the beast is familiar, and i take a little solace in that.

i'm a monster. there's no changing that. i can't deny it, refute it, or reverse it. it's who and what i am. i can't be the man i used to be. i can't be something i'm not…

moonbeams rule me. meat is my addiction, raw, red, blood on skin kinda meat. i've killed. i'll kill again. those moments come to me in murky dreams when i come back to myself. it's all just smeared ruin, gristle and bone, bodies without souls. i'm the perpetrator of all that suffering. i wish i could say that guilt is gone from my heart.

it's not. each time it happens, my heart swells. it oozes and it beats irregular. there's so much guilt in me i feel it may one day burst forth right along with the fangs and the fur.

the old maps used to say "here there be monsters" in the uncharted places of the world. those maps were right. here there be a monster.

a monster inside me…

Leech

she's warm, dripping with sweat, pupils dilated, a wetness sticking to her inner thighs. her hair falls against the pillow, a black cascade, her body as fragile as glass if i was so inclined to break it.

i've been here before. not with her, but with others. not in this room, but other rooms. sometimes i take them on a bed, or the floor, or pressed up against the wall with their desperate fingernails scratching into the cold stone of my back. years of this. decades of this. centuries piled atop centuries.

my only release is pleasure, hot, living flesh beneath my own bloodless hands. i taste them. i fuck them. i drink them dry. you ever feel like you're stuck in a loop where nothing changes? you wake up, you go to work, you eat, you go to sleep, you come home, and then you do it all over again. it's like you're bound. fate has dealt you an unfavorable hand and all you can do is go through the motions.

that's what it's like to live forever. that is immortality. that is sunless night after sunless night, throbbing throat after throbbing throat, everything you've ever loved fading and withering and aging while you remain perfectly the same.

it'll drive you crazy. it drove me crazy after the first hundred years or so. i've done it all. every depraved act of debauchery you've dreamed of but never acted upon out of fear.

i'm jealous of the world, because it is slowly dying while i am slowly living.

Apparition

the floorboards creak, the ceiling rains down dust, the windows are shattered and the moths come in with the night wind. this house was splendid once. no more. time is a thief, and it has stolen much from this place. a once proud mansion made into a revenant, a shadow of its former self.

the house is like me. forsaken. forgotten. alone with nothing but the spiders to keep me company, their webs decorated with husks that used to be flies. my footsteps are hollow thuds in empty hallways. a vagabond soul left behind, the mortal parts of me in the dirt, but the spirit still wandering, still staring out cracked windowpanes at the living.

i see them, but they never see me.

i used to be one of them. i used to laugh and smile like them. i used to love and hope like them. that's lost to me now. touch, taste, all those things i took for granted before this.

bodiless. invisible. a drifting leaf with no clear destination. i've found no door. i've been offered no other side. there was life, and then death, and then this.

is this damnation? is it hell? or am i just stuck in between, an unlucky shade that fell through the cracks?

i don't know.

i just wish they could see me one last time.

Witch

tail of newt. eyes of toad. mandrake root and leaves of weeping willows. boil it all together, make the tonic strong, strong enough to burn when it slides down the throat. they come to me when the doctors and the hospitals fail them.

i am useful, a necessary evil, old world magic competing with rising technology. my competitors are the cardiologists, the surgeons, and the machines that promise miracles. machines dictate the future. beeping, buzzing metal things that threaten to make me obsolete.

can a surgeon reach past the ribs and pull the black, charred cancer from the lungs?

can a cardiologist smear the heart with newfound love?

can the machines, those godless machines, reach into the planes of existence that mortals are never meant to see?

i hope it never comes to that. in the early years we were stoned, cast out, left to freeze or lifted up to burn. i give to men and women things that no one else can give them, and yet i remain shunned. they stone me with their eyes now, hard, unfeeling stares. although they do not put me to the stake in these modern times, it is their contempt that still manages to burn.

sometimes i draw the circles, speak the words, perform the invocations to bring the demons forth. i want nothing from them anymore. i just talk with them.

when you are as lonely as i, even a demon will do…

Wolf

the most important thing is control. you have to fight harder than you've ever fought in your life to maintain control when you are what i am. you are at war constantly, a shaggy soldier, and the battlefield is underneath your skin. your adversary is yourself. the darkest, most primal part of yourself.

imagine a tug of war, hands on the rope, one pair pink and human, the other pair paws with claws like black obsidian. some nights the man wins. other nights the beast reigns. and when the beast reigns, it's the man that is left to pick up the pieces.

torn, lacerated pieces that used to be people…

it never gets easier. you can't get close to people. you can't have a family. the man wants all the things that a man wants. the man wants a woman, a home, a life lived serene.

the wolf just wants to eat. he's not picky about his meals, and as long as they bleed and they scream, he'll devour without discrimination.

you have to build a cage in your mind. you have to forge shackles, make chains of your thoughts. your head becomes a fortress that keeps the wolf locked in, but when you bear this curse, the fortress keeps everyone else locked out too.

no home. no family. no connections to civilization.

just the deep, dark woods of solitude, and if you're lucky, the damage done there will be minimal.

Leech

blood everywhere. it's splattered across the wood, it's grimed under my fingernails, it's like gel slicking back my medium length blonde hair. i feel it dripping down my chin, a stream of plasma, my tongue slipping out to collect errant droplets.

it makes me feel alive again for a few short minutes. hot blood traveling through cold veins to feed a dead purple heart. i lick at the valleys of my palms, savoring the taste, relishing the differing blood types.

the dining room is dim, the dinner table stained a dark maroon. the father fell against the wall, his throat nothing but an open crater now. he struggled. it's good sport when they struggle.

the mother was like a doe facing down an eighteen wheeler on the highway. she never had a chance. i ripped apart her thighs and drank from the femoral. sweet like wine, a sensual death spasm. the children are broken brittle sacks beneath the table, empty eyed and pale as moonflowers. they were just appetizers.

how should i feel about this? the wholesale slaughter of an entire family. a perverse last supper, even the ceiling splashed with plasma and streaked in gritty gore.

i'll tell you how i feel. apathetic. vaguely bored. it was over too quickly, and now the fun fades. i lick my lips. i let the oceans that were their lives slosh around inside of me.

shame the fun never lasts.

Apparition

we don't pick our purgatories. afterlife is the epilogue to an unfinished story. chapters remain for me, i'm certain of that. no rewrites, though. life is a rough, messy draft, and sometimes no amount of polishing will make it presentable.

i'm in love with nostalgia, the times that once were, the moments that used to be. it's all that sustains me in this wispy nonexistence. memories like grainy photographs etched into the fibers of the soul.

the more time that passes, the more they fragment. do the dead suffer dementia? does it all become a whirlwind of footsteps, slammed doors, knocks on walls, just a routine with no perceivable purpose?

there was a boy and a girl. i remember the boy had blue eyes and the girl's smile brought the sunlight. they were mine. i made them in the womb of the body that once belonged to me. what were their names? do they live still?

bits and pieces come, but it's never enough. balloons floating up into the sky. a brush passing across the mane of a bowing horse. little hands seeking, hugging, and trusting.

i miss them. i miss everything here. candles became electric lights. horses became cars and trucks. letters written on paper became little notes that the living thumb into their mobile phones.

the world has changed. nothing remains the same.

except me.

Witch

i throw the bones, gleaning information from where they fall. the divination spell has consumed me lately, for some calamity lies ahead, but it's muddled and dark, and i squint until my head hurts, but still i do not see.

there is wrongness in the air. i hear it in the cawing of the crows, i smell it in the earth, i feel it across the bark of ancient oaks. an event approaches. something imperceptible but nevertheless looming.

my magic feels weak. sometimes the glamour flickers, young, lithe fingers becoming the gnarled digits of a hag. i have given everything for power, to perform delicious wonders, and yet the loss of power makes me feel like a kitten abandoned on the side of the road.

it's all centered on the calamity. this i know. to halt this degradation i must find the answers i seek. the bones won't show me, the tarot deck remains silent, and so a singular option remains.

i must prepare for a summoning. the circle must take shape, the altar must be built, the sacrifice must be generous. the things of the pit have knowledge, and it is desperate knowledge i now seek.

i will call to him.

he will whisper up from unknowable depths, just as he has whispered to me before.

Wolf

it's safer to keep moving. the backpacker life, hiking from trail to trail, cook by campfire, sleep beneath starlight, resupply in the towns only when the timing of the moon allows it.

i have never been a religious man, but a goddess has been forced upon me, and that goddess is the moon. she dictates every aspect of my life now. her crescent shape makes me itch. her half phase fills me up with strength, my bones becoming like iron, the muscles rounded steel. but it is when she is full, perfectly exposed and demanding worship—that is when i am unmade, a terror unleashed on this earth.

i avoid the thru-hikers and the trail families. i keep to the Appalachian Trail, but i veer off into uncharted wilderness when that bright whiteness rules the blackness of the sky. i am solitary, stoic, made forcibly shy like the black bears when they come across people.

if i do not shy away from people, then i will shred their lives into bloody ribbons. i choose isolation over devastation. my gift to them is my absence, a mercy in the time of tooth and claw. torn tents can be replaced. lacerated sleeping bags can be mended. inanimate objects can face destruction incarnate and nothing is lost.

when human beings face what i am, everything is lost.

Leech

it's the simple pleasures that make immortality slightly less mundane. a man needs hobbies. the denial of death offers lifetime after lifetime to pursue personal passions. make a kingdom of the world, and rule it as you see fit.

mine is a kingdom of excitement. i need the little thrills. as a shameless creature of excess, the thrills often precede the kills. she's thrilling as she grinds the pole, succulent and nubile, her flesh exposed for many hungry eyes in this little smoky club.

none hungrier than mine.

rosebud nipples, hips to shame Venus, eyes that sparkle and attract. her hair is fire, blazing red, an infernal halo. her eyes meet mine. they meet their match, and although her eyes attract, mine enchant.

she's curious. curiosity is my favorite. it kills many cats and many pretty young ones like her too. this pretty kitty doesn't know it yet, but her ninth life is up, and i've come to collect.

she leaves the stage, the music pounding, the crimson strobe lights shining down on her, making her veins pulse with the sugary ichor that animates everything that she is.

hello. she says it with a smirk, lips smeared black, black to match the silk of my shirt. i drain my glass of absinthe, a poor substitute for what i'm really craving.

all the best games start with hello...

Apparition

i watch the dust dance. sunlight comes and sunlight fades. night lasts forever. fireflies drift past the spiral staircase, some of them lost to the webs of opportunistic spiders. the lives of insects. do they matter? do i matter?

i sing sometimes but i can't hear myself. there's an old piano in the foyer, keys broken, bench hobbled, layers of plaster from the ceiling concealing most of what the instrument used to be. i tap the keys, sending discordant melodies through this house of nothing.

perhaps something here will find joy in the jagged music. the rats in the walls. the pigeons in the attic. a passing stranger with a heart that still beats and a life that has purpose.

i long for a stranger to wander in from the weedy vacancy beyond the windows. just to be in the presence of living, breathing flesh, something i once had and took for granted. not to harm that flesh, but to appreciate the majesty of it. to float near it, hear the breath in the lungs, to reach out with insubstantial fingertips and brush the cheek of a human being again.

my fingertips will pass through that skin, leaving nothing but a tingling chill, but to me it feels like coming in contact with an electric current. remembrance. beautiful moments that make up the grainy photo album of my dead thoughts.

those mental photographs are all that i have left. something worth clinging to…

Witch

black candles burn, inky wax like tendrils, the chalky circle scrawled around my seated form, a thin, membranous layer of protection, all that stands between me and what i call up from the dark spaces beneath this world and between others.

the syllables come, ancient tongue twisting, flick to summon, serpent recognizes serpent. the wind howls outside, making playthings of the trees. the vessel sits obediently in the center of the circle, a fat toad, skin a mottled brown, eyes listless, throat bobbing with a sort of grotesque rhythm.

it croaks mindlessly, a lilting chirp. it's mating season for the toads, that special time of nature's rebirth. the words compete with the wind now, my voice rising and falling, at once a whisper and a roar.

the one i call from the pit is a vain thing, and it loves to hear its name spoken. i invoke with that old name, that grimoire name, a series of guttural barks following the word of power. he is coming. i feel his ascent from the deep, the stale air of this room seeming suddenly thin, vacuumed up by his gathering presence.

clouds hide the moon, and in that perfect darkness, he has arrived. the flames of the candles sputter. the words die in the corridor of my throat.

the toad stares at me with vile cunning in its gaze. its body is fuller, contorting to contain the essence of the visitor. it croaks at me in familiar bubbling voice…

Wolf

the pines are a labyrinth, and in this labyrinth roams a minotaur. that minotaur is me. towering evergreens all around, limbs that reach at me, almost desperate to touch. i feel the forest in my bones now. this always happens before the change. a connection with this beautiful, damaged place we call mother earth.

she shows me her scars. she tells me the stories of them. she tells me she won't last, can't last, too many people, too much burden, crippling weight on the curves of her landscape.

my thoughts are a rambling mess inside of my head. i am moon drunk. the clouds hide that yellow disc in the sky for now, but soon they'll part. when those moonbeams fall, the beast will be reborn from within. there's no right place for that unbecoming, that remaking of body and soul.

i race through streets of oak and pine, alleys of rock and stream, searching for some little slice of desolation to fall to my knees and bay against the pain when my muscles start to rearrange. the pines part, showing an overgrown field in the middle of this vast nowhere. there's a meandering lane leading towards some distant civilization, but the house itself is a ruin.

sagging, abandoned, some great edifice open to the elements, a monument to rustic decay. it calls to me, those rotten walls, those singing, shattered windowpanes. that will be the place. the moonbeams are chasing me there, threatening to reveal what lies beneath.

this patient wolf will wait no longer.

Leech

i speak the language of this glamour girl, this thrill-seeking nymph with an insatiable hunger for life. we talk of sex, riches, travel, and even the meaning of the stars. her pierced nipples gleam beneath sheer black fabric, and as i build her up with pretty words, they press forward, yearning for freedom.

i have such promises to keep, and quarts to drink before i sleep. i already know what she'll taste like. she'll be a perfumed treat, skin tight with youth, throat unmarked, veins dripping from sweetness that centers in that naughty little heart of hers. she brags. she preens. she talks of sexual conquests and wild drug experimentation. i feign devoted interest.

internally i yawn. naïve little pseudo-rebel. how many of her kind have i devoured over the centuries? how many prattle on about the singular importance of their painfully short existences? too many. predictable creatures, these mortals. i read them like novels i've long since grown tired of.

in the great library of my lifetime, nothing surprises me anymore. there are no shocks to be had. i am perfectly desensitized to sights and acts that should be considered abhorrent. what is sin but exploration?

i do still love to explore…

she's still talking. the highway races past, the top down on her ruby-red convertible. she's speeding dangerously, almost racing to beat the devil. too late for that…because a devil rides beside her.

Apparition

do spirits dream? surely i am lost in some surreal slumber. how else can i account for the stranger that has staggered in from the wilderness? it is a man, but he must be wounded, in terrible pain, for he screams, he grunts, his entire body seems to seize with some internal torment.

i long to wet a cool rag and place it across his steaming brow, but such niceties are reserved for the living. i can do nothing but watch him writhe, unseen, invisible, a spectator with the inability to act. it is terribly frustrating, for some great malady infects this man, the fits becoming more violent, the sounds from his throat so wretched and anguished that he sounds more bestial with each passing moment.

is he a shivering epileptic? could he be a madman, some pitiful nomad with a broken brain? he tears at his clothes, ripping them from his body, his musculature soaked in sweat and smelling vaguely canine. his mouth stretches in his bearded visage, a ragged hole voicing whatever horrible illness plagues his existence.

i watch in ghostly silence, his fingernails digging at the floorboards, his skin seeming flushed and irritated, any sense of self evaporating from his tortured expression. surely he must be some escaped invalid from the sanitarium in the hills to the south?

his limbs seem longer. his teeth seem sharper. what is that coarse black hair sprouting from his twisted spine? the eyes. oh god, why are his eyes glowing like burning lanterns in the sockets…

Witch

"now you call? lonesome eons pass, but it is not want that calls me, it is desperation."

the eyes of the toad roll over my face with demonic indifference.

"i call with questions."

"what else? always questions. the tree of knowledge has been picked clean by the grubby hands of mankind. none more guilty than the whores of lucifer, seeking always more like a child begging for seconds…"

"lucifer is your master, and it is to him that you and i both owe our good fortune."

"fortune is futile in the pit, woman. you practitioners of the black arts will learn that when you come to dwell where i dwell."

"i wish not to offend. i seek only answers. i feel that something waits on the horizon, some colossal end. unsettling premonitions come, but all is fire and ash, and nothing can be understood from it."

"have you not tasted the gifts of the pit for years beyond years? false youth? loyal familiars? totems to beguile and spells to eviscerate? avarice blinds you. the answer drifts in the fire and ash, and i'll give you no more."

the tongue of the toad flicks from the gaping mouth to swallow a buzzing fly. it regards me with bulging idiot eyes, the presence having already departed, leaving nothing behind but hollowness and smoke from extinguished candles.

Wolf

i awaken to devastation, a common occurrence for me. my head is foggy, my human thoughts retaking the fading instincts of the beast. it's something i call the turn hangover, a general feeling of mugginess that will take time to dissipate.

i'm splayed out on a ratty couch in a sprawling foyer. the walls bear fresh claw marks, the banisters of the staircase gnawed and chewed down to splinters. a tornado swept through this place last night, and that tornado was me. there are no shredded bodies lying at my feet, so that gives me a modicum of solace. only the house itself felt the wrath of the wolf.

sunlight slants in through broken windows, and lazy monarch butterflies float in with the breeze, their yellow wings flashing as they perform aerial acrobatics. i roll onto my back and watch the butterflies twirl and explore the dusty innards of this ruin. my pack lies near the coach, my clothes in an untidy pile near it.

i'm horribly sore, but that is expected, a byproduct of your entire anatomy twisting and contorting into something entirely new. even in human form my sense of smell is incredible, and the aromas of this forgotten mansion tingle in my nostrils. mildew. rotting wood. nesting vermin and hidden insects. there's a smell underneath though, something that puzzles me.

it's a wispy scent, something ethereal and intangible. it seems so close, almost hovering over me. it is both fresh and infinitely formless. it makes me feel that i'm not alone here after all…

Leech

have you ever pinched a vibrant firefly between your fingertips and placed it into a glass jar? be honest. many have. morbid curiosity compels you to capture that glow, make that incandescence your own. you know the firefly is a lesser being, and you realize that bottling it up will kill it sooner or later, but you have this selfish desire to keep the light flickering as long as possible for your own personal amusement.

i suppose that's why i haven't drained her dry yet. this vivacious, glowing, sinuous dancer of the graveyard hours. as a fellow predatory being, i identify most with the big cats, because playing with my food seems to make it all the more savory. it's fun to play with this one. we lie on our backs in some overgrown meadow, crickets chirping, starlight baptizing us, the sound of the car radio lulling us into fanciful imaginings.

she muses about big cities and even bigger dreams. outwardly i encourage her musings, while inwardly i muse about sucking down every last drop of her dreams right along with her steaming plasma. she carries the light of wanderlust inside of her, and that particular taste has always been a favorite of mine. it's like taking in the essence of all the roads she'll never travel and all the oceans she'll never reach and all the people she'll never meet.

she asks me if i've traveled. a little, i tell her. the truth is i've explored this globe from end to end, and it holds no secrets from me in my advanced age. every road a retread, every bustling metropolis a familiar haunt…

Apparition

what is this bearded thing with his sad eyes
and his warm, oven-like skin? an animal? a man?
some unnatural blending of the two? the
previous night was an aberration. it was like a
ticket to the sideshow tent in a traveling
carnival. surely it was all some illusion, some
trickery, but why here, in this house of broken
boards and sagging walls?

there is no audience here but me, and even if i
were to applaud with shock or gasp with fright,
the poor devil would never even hear it. i
glided close to the staircase while he was
wolfish and wild, the shadow of fear lingering
within even though such a brute could do no
harm to a bodiless being like me.

but when slumber overtook him i watched his
tortured flesh consume the animal and spit
forth the man once again. he lay there in a
pool of perspiration, exhausted and hollow-eyed,
his breathing that of a man who had just
conquered the summit of some high mountain.

he is the first visitor i've had in a long,
long time. i left the comfort of the staircase,
daring to get close to him, to let these foggy,
forgotten fingertips trace the curve of one
bearded cheek. his thick lashes. his brooding
brow. an outdoorsman through and through, his
skin kissed by sun and wind.

when his eyes flutter open, dark and deep,
dazzling orbs that seem so thoughtful and
pained, i get the queerest idea that he senses
me. surely that cannot be. surely he cannot see
my wilting white dress, and surely he cannot
hear the sigh of a shade. and yet, this visitor
seems so different from all the rest…

Witch

everything aches. it takes great energy to call up the ones from the pit, a strenuous mental and physical exercise, and afterwards the body is sore and sickly for days at a time. there's a hollow ache in the mouth, a sensation like my teeth are throbbing, the enamel feeling brittle and sharp against the gums.

the pain is worth it when i'm given concrete answers, but so often the infernal visitors spit out riddles and lies, and it is hard to find the bits and pieces of truth hidden in those spoken ciphers.

this time was especially frustrating, maybe because i'm so much older and long disconnected from invocations, and even the serpents i once called my kin seem to sense that the life animating these wasted bones may flicker out at any moment. even with magic of the blackest sort, i cannot escape the fragility of the human body i inhabit.

i am a woman withered, a woman well past her expected years, and perhaps i should be concerned more with my own failing state instead of the premonition of some gray, horrible cloud on a distant horizon.

i cannot shake it, though. i turned to spells and potions because knowledge is the rawest form of power, and i cannot rest until i know the nature of what fate has in store for this world.

even now, my addiction to knowledge drives me, and it will not be satiated until i have a proper fix…

Wolf

i don't know why i linger in this house. i should pack up and go. there's nothing for me here but dirty floorboards and twirling shadows. the rooms are barren, the ceiling rotting, the walls crumbling to expose the skeletal frame that hides behind them.

it's clear that the world has left this place behind, so why can't i? i don't know. there's a sense of desperate attention that seems to circle me. i almost imagine that i hear a voice, some long lost whisper, begging me to stay a little longer, imploring me to see past the ruin to a time when this mansion was a glory to behold.

i wish i could. i feel eyes on me—a woman's eyes—but there is no woman here. i even smell her, a scent like smooth bare feet and the fabric of a dress that once rested among wildflowers. she must be some remnant from a dream, a barely conceived form that took root in my mind during the deep sleep after man retakes wolf.

i brush my hands against worm-eaten banisters. my boots clomp across shattered pieces of glass, little shards of windows, the sunlight glinting off of them. i take a great circular staircase up to the second floor, scenting but never seeing, feeling a yearning that can't be properly explained, a yearning that i'm unable to return.

this house is a part of a story, that much i know. but whose story?

Leech

she's a faucet now, and she pours sublime red ichor from wounds all over her body. i've made an artistic piece of her, the scarlet dahlia, and oh how i relish the starlight on my back as i wet my fangs over and over again in flesh that is supple with sin.

i love to watch their eyes when i steal away their fluttering moth-lives. it's glassy theater in the irises, a tragedy playing out, everything slipping away so slowly, totally unplanned, a glimmer of disbelief mingling with the black holes of fear that her pupils have transformed into.

she will never dance again. she will never laugh again. she will never lust, or love, or taste the fruits of life again. i bleed her intimately, drawing out her essence in deep, rich mouthfuls. there's not a single square of flesh on this unfortunate girl that does not bear teeth marks. i've tasted all parts, each more delectable than the last.

she's my pretty painting, wheezing and fading, but she only coughs a little when i break her ribs apart and smear her still beating heart with a carnal kiss. it's our last kiss. her last kiss. i tongue the arteries, licking at the aorta, sucking down the meaty blackish blood of her brave little organ.

and just like that, she's gone. she's given me all she has, every drop, and i'll always remember her for that. i lap the last stains of scarlet from her before throwing the husk of her body behind me, the torso rolling through meadow grass. kind of her to leave such a lavish car behind...

Apparition

i wish i could properly define the end of existence. it's hard to explain being someone, a living thing connected to a living universe, and then the transition—or downfall—into this world of shades of gray. the first thing i noticed was the quiet emptiness. it's a silence so profound that it oppresses you. i often feel suffocated by all this silence even though i lost my lungs when my corpse went into the coffin.

sleep is the prelude before death, a few opening acts to prepare one for the vast darkness waiting at the end of life's personal path. the curtains flutter and briefly close when you sleep, but they always reopen with the dawn. the curtains close forever when death comes calling. the scythe sweeps you off the stage, and your brief moment in the spotlight is over before you ever truly had the chance to savor it.

i wish i had savored it more. if i knew how finite my time was, i would have taken more risks, explored more distant lands, and made every effort possible to leave my mark behind in the history books. i took time for granted, and the hands of the clock remained merciless. they stop for no one, and they remember every heartbeat…

i'm screaming now, begging to be heard, the raggedy remnants of curtains blowing ever so delicately in the wind of my screams. it seems that his ears perk up, but is it just wishful thinking?

does he truly hear me?

Witch

i hate the inability to find the answers that i seek. there's rage taking root inside, a slow burn, the brewing of an internal cauldron that sloshes with malevolent thoughts. i want to kill something. i want to pluck the eyes out of something innocent and force that innocent thing to keep on living for my own personal entertainment.

i am made impotent by these uncooperative devils, my magic useless, my incantations nothing but hollow words in a dirty hovel. it's quiet, needling torment. i am goaded into hateful ruminations due solely to the fact that i'm not being given the answers that i seek.

these devils know much, but they are prickly creatures, and to draw the truth from one of them is akin to pulling a bloody wisdom tooth from the mouth, a violent root canal with nerve tissue still trailing from the wound.

my mind has limits, it is not bottomless, and if the space continues to fill with hatred, i fear it will spill over soon. it will drip down the sides of my skull like red, viscous wax, and it will scald every single entity i come into contact with.

a witch is a glutton for power, and if denied for too long, the glutton is forced to devour with impunity. these emotions rule me, reminding me of my own human fragility, a mind trapped in a body that quakes with tremors of barely defined fury.

this cannot go on.

Wolf

the walls seem to press in on me, seeking some form of paltry embrace. there are words in the ragged desolation, unintelligible whispers drifting up from the skeletal remnants of a bed frame. maybe it's my own preternatural gifts working against me, but the very air of this room feels alive, a constantly whirling breeze pricking my flesh and playing across my skin with the softness of lithe fingertips on piano keys.

dead brown leaves from autumns long since past seem to float in the room, that wind a constant thing, animating multiple pieces of detritus. dirt, bird feathers, animal fur, specks of mold, all of it swirling around me, and for the briefest of moments it seems almost like a female figure beckons from this spinning wind tunnel, her fingers raven feathers, her eyes bits of discarded costume jewelry, her lips pouting leaves that struggle against insubstantiality.

i feel claustrophobic. a large part of me is an animal, and the worst thing for an animal is the idea of being caged against its will. it's the large, open spaces that give me solace. it's the meadows without end and the woodlands that defy civilization. there's a force in this house, a tangible force, but it begs for a sort of rudimentary companionship that i'm incapable of returning.

there's a beast in my heart, and the beast rejects the walls in favor of the wild.

i turn to leave…i turn back towards the comfort of the wild…

Leech

i love a good distraction. i'm always looking for them, my keen eyes crawling over a world that's ripe with possibilities. a family torn apart one by one while forced to watch each other die. that's a distraction. a supple stripper drained to the last sweet drop, all the while thinking she's destined for great and special things, when in actuality she's destined to nourish a dead-but-dashing apex predator. major distraction.

these distractions exist solely to amuse me. i control the outcome of their otherwise dull, monotonous existences, their predictable lives ending at the hands and fangs of a wholly unpredictable night creature.

i've always appreciated control. the idea that you are master and commander of another living, thinking, feeling organism, and since they are lesser organisms, they have no choice but to submit to whatever dark whims you can dream up. they are slaves to torment, bleeding sacks to rupture and ruin, nothing but puppets of dangling defeatism, and it should honor them that i even take an interest in cutting at their strings.

when you see an insect crawling across the ground, the sight of it pathetic and offensive, you don't think twice about smashing your boot down and crushing it into a brittle paste. it's an unimportant life form. if you are a god in comparison to such a life form, why not be cruel and have a little fun?

even gods grow bored. even gods need recreation…

Apparition

he's going now, his pack affixed to his shoulders, those muddy boots trudging towards the front door. i will him to stop. i will him to understand, but i am but a whirling nothing, and i am forced to watch this mysterious visitor departing.

his nostrils expand, seeming to scent something in the place, but the scent is a puzzle to him, and he cannot or will not stay to solve it. this prison of walls and rot seems almost to laugh at me, my hope for companionship slipping through my fingers like worthless ectoplasm. all that will remain when he leaves is the solitary confinement of this purgatory, and it could be years before another living soul finds this barren place.

he reaches the door, heavy hands reaching out to touch the splintered wood. he seems almost to hesitate, looking back, eyes gleaming in that sad, bearded face. i beg him to see me. i weep for him to sense just the most illusory idea of what i am and why i'm here. he cannot see, he cannot hear, and he cannot find it in himself to know.

he sighs, his body exiting the threshold, his living, breathing tissue moving through the meadow. how can i explain the desperation of this? he's beyond my barrier now, and i am helpless to follow. all i can do is scream, but my screams produce no sound, only wind in the distant trees. i fall to my knees, knees that no longer exist, and i reach for him.

i reach for the trees that consume him.

i am too late. the man from the woods is gone.

Witch

denial is a bitter seed lodged in the throat, but it's there all the same. no answers. no promises of future longevity. the ones in the pit are like little bully boys that would rather spit on you and pull your hair as opposed to offering real assistance.

i boil the stew, just a malnourished rabbit caught in a snare, nothing bewitching about it. it'll taste thin and stale, but i'll crunch down all the tiny brittle bones regardless. a paltry meal for a sulking crone, but i feel no shame in the sulking. is it so wrong to cling to youth? is it a sin to covet knowledge? we are beasts of great curiosity, and it is the purest pleasure to learn. and that which is forbidden to learn is the greatest prize of all.

i twist the wooden spoon, tapping against lumpy gray meat with the steam of the water kissing my face, and that is when it happens. that is when the vision comes roaring through my brain, a wonderful locomotive bringing colors, shapes, and prophetic images.

i see flashes of flat, endless land. wild horses galloping across sagebrush. a sky that seems so spectacularly blue. abandoned oil derricks rusting and falling. but this emptiness is not entirely empty.

there is a house. it defies the desolation around it, a great, sprawling castle of a structure. i see libraries within, great shelves filled with rare arcane tomes. spells lost to time. incantations i've always sought in vain. i see a mirror, and i'm there in the reflection. eternally young, sleek brown hair and supple skin. the House of Knowledge…

Wolf

i couldn't stay there. that wasted old place full of broken things. it reminded me too much of myself. a broken man trying to find his way in a world that the wolf always seeks to break even more. but was there someone there? someone reaching and hoping i'd stay?

no. there was nothing there. just the imaginings of a mind that has grown insular in solitude. i must never forget my rules. always keep moving, never put down roots, ensure that the damage you do is as minimal as possible. stay away from people, for you have nothing to offer them but suffering.

i repeat these rules silently to myself as i make camp beneath the pines. no moon tonight, and that is a mercy. just clouds above and stars that grant me all the shine they can.

i nestle down into the sleeping bag, the campfire blazing to my left. i stare up at the stars, so many dark constellations. they seem to blend together. something is happening. i'm seeing things in the stars. what the hell is—

a sky that lasts forever. it is so blue, so much sun, and all beneath it is warm. desert land, remote, just horizon meeting horizon. coyotes skulk and pronghorn antelopes graze together across the featureless fathoms.

there is a house. some massive lodge built from logs, the chimney sending up smoke tendrils, the door like the vast mouth of a cave. all the people i've ever hurt stand in front of it, waving and welcoming, no longer bleeding carcasses. a home that will accept me. the House of Redemption…

Leech

i'm driving in the dead dancer's car, and it seems the highways of the night are full of possibilities. i'm in the mood for a big city. i want lights, voices, a cacophony of vice and victims. i want something a little stained, dirtied by age and degradation. Detroit sounds good.

i am a lazy lion after glutting itself on a satisfying meal, and i feel like napping for awhile. the long slumber always revitalizes me. i'll find a derelict house on a derelict street and crawl down into the lowest ground level and sleep for a year or two. Detroit has no shortage of slums, and i'll awake fresh and fetching, eager to taste all the city has to offer. blood, sex, and drugs…these are a few of my favorite things.

my hand tightens on the wheel, my mind made up on a destination, but why are my thoughts suddenly buzzing in my head? there is a mental onslaught occurring. i'm seeing…

the hidden haven in the Big Empty. a shining skyscraper jutting up from flat earth. there's a penthouse at the top, and oh what pleasures reside there. a carved obsidian fountain spouting virgin blood. nubile women balled together like serpents on scarlet sheets, all pink nipples and milky thighs. medieval torture devices along each corridor, the very sight of them enough to harden the cock. gibbets, judas cradles, pears of anguish, and breaking wheels…

a pleasure palace, a funhouse, a place to fuck and kill and drink every blood type on the market. this wonderful place. this wonderful vision. the House of Flesh & Blood…

Apparition

i am alone. if a word defines me, that word is alone. i drift past walls that i've grown so tired of. i linger in front of a cold fireplace that has forgotten how to burn. the floorboards don't even creak for me, because my footsteps carry no weight. another visitor gone. a potential friend, a sympathetic ear for a dead voice, gone, swallowed by the wilderness.

and so i pace and float through worthless rooms, the cabin fever so severe that it threatens to drive me mad. can a ghost go mad? can a specter lose the mind it no longer has? i don't know, but perhaps it would be better if madness did come.

it would be better than this horrible awareness. the rational thought that this is all there is, just pointless plodding in pointless purgatory. i would tear out my hair and rip my dress to pieces if it were possible, but these parts of me are just wispy facsimiles, nothing but the faded photograph version of what and who i used to be.

once again the cold fireplace, just ash and cinders. i stare into it. why bother? there's no fire there. but…there is a fire. it comes suddenly out of nowhere, not in the fireplace, but in my thoughts. bright, burning images…

my house—or a mansion much like it—in a field of sagebrush. not a ruin, but a perfect copy of what it once was transplanted to some flat piece of land. beautiful, regal, full to the brim with smiling faces. they all see me. not the ghost of me, but the living, breathing me, my flesh mine again. my body mine again, and what bliss. it's there…in the House of Life…

Witch

i've tried each spell available to me to ascertain the source of the vision. it did not come from those that dwell in the pit. it's untraceable, but i feel in my bones that it is an actual place. that house exists. i can still smell the eldritch pages of those tomes and scrolls, my ticket to lost magic that i've never experienced before.

it's been so long since i've traveled. i pack up my meager possessions and take hold of my gnarled walking staff. there's nothing left for me in this hovel. if i stay here walking this dirt floor and watching the mushrooms grow in the dank corners then fragility will claim me sooner rather than later, and then it's all over.

the house in the sagebrush is my only chance. it's thousands of miles away, but witches travel fast, and witches have their ways. no more fetid potions to abort the unborn for scared teenagers. no more mandrake root tea to peddle to the infirm. my time here is finished, and the last great journey awaits.

i work the last vestiges of my glamour, taking on the shape of the girl i used to be, all silky brown hair and big, innocent doe eyes. the crone hidden beneath false flesh, because a woman's looks will get her far on the roads to come.

i kick at the embers beneath the boiling pot, and soon the straw of my bedding catches. the flames have their way. let it burn, let it blacken, let the inferno swallow it all.

Wyoming calls to me…and so i go.

Wolf

i thought this was all my life would ever be now. i am accursed, so it's inevitable that i must walk the accursed path. a bleak, honest resignation, but those pictures in the stars have changed everything. there is a glimmer of hope on some distant horizon. the wolf sniffs at it mistrustfully, but the man has made his choice.

i'll find that house. my heart tells me that it's real, not some fantasy or fever dream, but a place in the world that can actually help me to make some kind of sense of my own curse. i close my eyes, the pictures like memories fresh in my head.

chimney smoke. polished log walls. fresh, open air and glorious serenity. people that understand, people that know, but most importantly, people that forgive. i hate the things i've done. i hate myself for harming those that never deserved harm. there must be some way to cage the wolf permanently, to dull his canines and clip his claws. if there is a way, i'll find it in the Big Empty.

i'll take the mountain trails as far as i can by foot and find some transportation in one of the towns. my heart will lead me to the house, and somewhere in that vast, overlooked country i'll find what i'm looking for.

i don't know what the house is. i don't know why it chose me. i do not question it. perhaps a sanctuary for the monster inside. perhaps a way to euthanize the monster inside.

i'll find out when i get there.

Leech

i lost control of the car when the waking dream hit. it spun in a full 360 before coming to rest in the center of the road, the stink of burning rubber invading my nostrils. fuck it. i would have gladly allowed the car to flip a hundred times just to have those delicious recollections rolling through my mind.

blood everlasting. a tidal wave for the tongue. tits and cunt to flick, tease, and slowly devour. human bodies ripe for despair, a literal kingdom in a scrubby desert. i don't care who sent the vision. it's the most interesting thing that's happened to me in at least a century or two.

that palace needs a prince, and who better than i? the stink of that rich, flowing blood will lead me there. i'll come upon it in darkness, as i come upon all things, and that black, crooked skyscraper will yield all the dripping delights to me.

Wyoming is a bore, nothing to see, nothing to do, but if such a hedonistic house is to be found there, i'll make my own fun along the way. i'll bleed out a few wild horses and paint the plains in their ruptured parts, a little marked trail for others of my kind to find the way.

Detroit can wait. the long slumber can wait. suddenly i'm wide awake and looking to luxuriate in this den of promised violence. i spin the steering wheel and turn the car around, blazing off in the opposite direction.

Big Empty, here i come...

Apparition

the threshold mocks me. that gaping doorway to the meadow beyond, so close, nothing but a few steps out of the foyer. it has always seemed impenetrable. the nature of a ghostly existence seems to dictate that you are anchored to a specific place or object, and i do not know if it's possible to pull that anchor free.

each time i've tried to leave, i'm pushed back by a light, unseen breeze. it's an elastic barrier, some thin veil that conceals the wide world out there from the claustrophobic world in here. i'm not meant to leave. whatever fates decided that my specter would live on after me also locked me up in this prison of memories.

i'd usually just give up. i'd return to aimless wandering, hopeless and resigned to something that i cannot change. not this time. there's life waiting for me in that house in Wyoming. i don't know what sent the vision of that house to me. i do not care. perhaps a devil, a deity, or something else entirely. it is the promise that matters. a return to flesh, and a second chance at the mortal coil. this bolsters my will. i am made stubborn at the thought of finding this house full of life and departing this house full of death.

i press against the threshold. it pushes back, but i press harder. my entire bodiless form seems like it's being wedged through an invisible filter, something meant to contain for eternity. i scream with a voice that makes no sound. i flail out with arms that are no longer there, kicking with legs that don't exist. i'm breaking through. i fall forward into wildflowers. i am out. i am in the world…

Witch

the world hasn't changed since the last time i ventured abroad. it's the same churning, boiling ball of people. it's just smog, exhaust, body odor and a race that is defined by mindless distractions. beeping phones. flickering screens. anything to draw attention away from the shrieking, dying earth that lies beneath their feet.

men are the same. men have always been the same. they are predictable meatbags with lolling tongues, and if you show them a little leg and a loquacious wink, they are putty to be formed into any shape you choose. my glamour always does the trick. a beautiful woman is a man's perfect ruin, and how willing they are to throw themselves into false flesh.

i walked the roads, those bisecting interstates that rule the country now. the ones in the big trucks are the easiest prey. lonely souls far from home, so eager to play the scruffy hero to the damsel in roadside distress. you weave a story just as you weave a spell. car trouble, far from home, whatever shall i do?

a hero comes along with a crooked smile and a pinch of chewing tobacco tucked behind his bottom lip. he rides no white steed, but his eighteen wheeler will do. he is called joe. joe has two children and a thin little wife at home in Virginia. joe's left eye twitches and his graying hair is greasy beneath his baseball cap.

a lonely soul with a low IQ, just a big, dumb dog eager to please a pretty face. he's my ticket to the Big Empty. my escort to the house across the plains. oh yes. joe will do just fine…

Wolf

it's been a long time since i've left the woods. the loamy scent of the soil being crunched underfoot and the wind floating through the leaves has been music to soothe my tortured heart. it's better to be what i am in the remote regions of the world. the cities and the towns worry me, not because i fear civilization, but because i fear the damage i can inflict upon civilization.

i know what i am. when that moon rises, i am a killing machine, nothing more, nothing less. when the incisors grow and the canines elongate, all is lost for those that encounter me. i have to play this right. i keep a battered old calendar and farmer's almanac in my pack, and those will serve me well as this search begins.

i must always be aware of the lunar phases, the waxing and the waning of cruel mother moon. she only brings death when she comes. the only gift she's ever given me is the gift of guilt, and if this house really exists, maybe i'll finally find a way to reverse and return a gift that i never wanted in the first place.

i do a little work here and there before i go. i chop wood, i wash dishes, and i bartend at shithole dives full of lumberjacks and bikers. once i've got enough money to get me well on my way, it doesn't take much to haggle with one of the bikers for a suitable chopper that'll see me through. it's a 1929 Triumph, perfectly maintained, all gleaming metal and glossy black.

she'll ride fast and powerful, and the wolf inside will like that. it'll keep him docile for awhile. it's time to leave the pines behind.

Leech

i stare down at a puddle of sugary soda in a rest stop parking lot. it draws moths and other little winged night insects, proboscis after proboscis slurping up the brownish liquid that clings to the styrofoam cup. i'm reminded of myself in some ways. always slurping my way through immortality, drink after drink, seeking new flavors to tantalize the undead taste buds.

i'm also reminded of my childhood as i stare down at the moths bathed in the amber glow of sodium-vapor lamps. a boyhood long before the turn. it seems so misty now, like the memories belong to someone else, dulled by lifetime after lifetime. when i was alive as a boy, my great joy was extinguishing the lives of things smaller than me. it started with the insects.

salt for slugs. hair spray and a zippo lighter for ant hills. safety pins to stab into beetles while watching them writhe, their legs crawling against nothing but air. i was a little vlad even then, i suppose, an impaler of insects and a conqueror of hive nations. i'd tear the wings from butterflies and piss on their mutilated bodies. once i grew a bit older i begged mommy and daddy for pets, and i graduated to larger game. suffice is to say, those pets never lasted... i guess immorality hasn't changed me much. my inner child lives still, and he delights in the bloodless corpse at my feet, one chubby hand still holding that styrofoam cup. just an unlucky traveler who chose the wrong rest stop to sip his soda pop. but this is nothing compared to what awaits me. mild foreplay before the raw, red ravages of the house ahead.

Apparition

i'm out. i can't believe i'm out. i look up,
seeing the world as i remember it, but
everything shrouded in fog, and with the fog
comes a constant rain. i suppose this is the
world for a remnant, but i feel no despair. i
dance my formless form in rainfall that never
touches me, the mist that surrounds me much
like the mist of my own limbs.

there are still wildflowers. i hear the distant
chirp of songbirds and the rustling of a family
of deer on the edge of the forest. this is
freedom from the crumbling mansion at my back.
whatever cord that tied me there is severed,
and now i'm permitted to roam. perhaps it is
the pull of the house that has granted me this
unshackling. perhaps it was my own will alone
that helped me break through to the other side,
this side, this wonderful wide open side.

i take one last look at the rotting edifice
that stands behind me. it looks especially
forsaken now, uninhabited even by lingering
ghosts. its time has run out, and soon the
wilderness will grow inward and eat up whatever
is left of the walls.

i will not miss this place, this painful
reminder of life stolen, just a purgatorial
circle that did nothing but taunt and enslave
me. this is my past, just as dead as me, and my
future is the house, my future is life. an end
to bodiless movements and unheard words. i'll
speak again. i'll touch again. i'll be flesh
again. i float towards my future, and i float
towards the renewal of life.

Witch

joe drinks black coffee, no cream, lukewarm and swirling. joe talks about his brat children and his worthless wife, and i feign the barest of interest. joe talks about the long nights on the road and the time spent away from his family. i'd like to open up the hood of joe's big rig and place his flabby bloodhound face against the radiator until it melts into a pool of yellow fat, charred bone, and bubbling blood.

but not yet. i need him a bit longer. mostly i'm interested in the landscapes that fly by in the passenger side window. forests. deserts. sometimes burning sun, sometimes torrential rain, and sometimes falling snow. each time i permit myself to sleep it seems i awaken in a new state and a new climate. it's like i'm traveling through different worlds, each one lacking, because the only world i want harbors a house to bolster my magic.

still far away, but closer than i was before. i give ol' joe little flashes of motivation from time to time to keep him rolling onward. a hand brushed against his meaty bicep. a sparkling smile and a fluttering of lashes. it doesn't take much to please this pathetic mongrel, and he'll remain wrapped around my little finger for the duration of the drive.

he can take me only as far as Colorado. he'll be unloading there and then starting for home. i don't think joe will be returning home. i think joe will make a fitting sacrifice for those in the pit, an offering to them so that they'll favor me in the last legs of my journey.

a woman's work is never done.

Wolf

the open road feels right. i've trimmed the hair and the beard, a passable human again instead of some raggedy vagabond that looks like he hasn't bathed in years. the handlebars feel good gripped in my calloused hands, and the roar of the motorcycle's engine has the intended effect. the beast is soothed. he is curled up inside, content for now, the purring of the bike like a lullaby to him.

i rent cheap hotel rooms and eat alone in diners that never close. i keep the farmer's almanac with me always, the lunar calendar dog-eared and smudged in oily fingerprints. i'm making good time, but i don't know if i can reach the house before the moon grows full again. i need to be ready for that. i'm taking the back roads just to be safe, but even these roads lead past sparse communities.

i'll need to find a turning place. i can't risk running wild where i am now. the wilderness i came from was desolate and vast, but it's not the same out here. when i find a place, i'll have to use the chains again. it's been a long time since i've used the chains. they are a last resort, a temporary solution when the change comes.

they don't always work. 80% of the time they keep the wolf's rage shackled, but there have been moments where he'll bite himself bloody just to get free. other times he has torn them from whatever anchor i bolted them against.

it is a gamble, but isn't this entire trip a gamble?

Leech

it's sweltering hot in Texas. i fancy a dip on this wonderful road trip, and the lake on the outskirts of this dairy farm will do just fine. it's of no real consequence that i have two giggling, drunken college girls following along behind me, clomping along in their daisy dukes, their plump ass cheeks looking oh so ripe in torn short-shorts. one is petite with apple cheeks, the other tall and bottle-blonde, her legs like that of a mare.

apparently a handsome face and handsome words will get you far at a country western bar. they pull at their clothing, eager to go skinny dipping, so desperate to appear adventurous to this stranger from parts unknown. i follow their lead. i let my white slacks fall, and i allow the girls to peel the white blazer from my shoulders. i like their smell. i can almost taste the little beads of sweat that have collected around the lips of their cunts. bellies full of liquor, eyes full of lust, veins pumping with a powerful flow. i have a game where i try to guess their blood alcohol content when i drain them dry. what will it be for these two fillies, then? time will tell.

into the water we go, splashing, diving, touching and playing. they remain near the surface, but i go down deep. they get worried. they wonder what became of their daring companion. they don't have to wait long. i burst upwards and drag them down, our drunken damsels flailing and kicking at me with their pedicured toes. a mixture of water and blood pours into their lungs. soon the lake is red.

i float in a scarlet hot tub of my own making.

Apparition

i can move much faster out here in the open. i do not walk as the living do, instead i levitate across the earth, moving through endless rain and fog. i am bodiless and so i am tireless, able to travel day and night, gaining ground with each passing second. all for the house that is promised…

i linger for awhile in the bustling cities, watching the gears of life still turning all around me. cars. trains. women walking dogs and men with newspapers tucked beneath their arms. they all come and go in the mist, moving about their personal paths without the slightest idea that i am there admiring them.

i hope they appreciate what they have. it is a precious thing, this life. it's a grainy photograph that does not last, but perhaps there is a chance to make that photograph vibrant again. a slim possibility to let the colors and images leap forth and draw the eye once again.

that's all i want. just a second chance. can you give me that, beautiful house in the Big Empty? can you let me touch a human face again with nimble fingers? can you let me feel this rain on my skin and catch the droplets in open palms?

i know you can. i believe in you.

i have faith in the house. a dream come true, and a dream too long denied. what waits behind your walls?

resurrection.

Witch

we're somewhere in Kansas. cornfields stretched across every available horizon. joe is waxing poetic about the vista, the ability to see flat landscape everywhere you look. it's about as impressive as watching a snail crawl across a stone. i'm pretending to listen when the mental shockwave hits.

the cornfield burns away, the stalks torn from the dirt and turning to ash. that castle of a house pushes up from the soil, battlements, towers, and rooms for eternal exploration. i'm flying towards it, the scent of ancient books in my nostrils and the taste of knowledge sliding blissfully down my throat.

i see myself draining some violet potion, my skin becoming supple, my wrinkles tightening, my heart growing strong and youthful again. no glamour necessary. the house provides. i see the ones from the pit cowering in the shadows around me, no longer masters i must cater to, but simpering servants that exist only to carry out my orders.

my hair whips wildly about my shoulders, silky with deep roots. thousands of bottles and jars line the shelves, a bottomless well of incantations, remedies, and my favorite of all, curses. curses to make the eyeballs bleed. curses to make the genitals turn black and rot. a curse for every day, a curse for every atrocious way, and they'll all be mine.

the house will be mine.

the vision fades slowly. joe said my eyes rolled back into my head. joe said i had a fit.

Wolf

there's nothing but the remnants of a stone foundation, a crumbling chimney, and the oldest birch i've ever seen. the birch much have grown right up through the living room when this little building once stood. it's a humongous tree, the bark white and weathered, branches reaching up towards the sky as though the birch fears the sun's abandonment.

it will be here, and it must be now. there are no people or houses for miles around. just this hill and this tree, and that's all the company i intend to keep on this night that will soon be moonlit. i take hold of the chains and wrap them around my body, crisscrossing beneath arms and legs. i wrap the heaviest portion of the chain around the trunk of the birch, and i double it just in case. the padlock falls against my bare chest, vaguely cool, metal on skin.

now i wait. only another hour or so. i can feel him inside, pacing and growling in the far back of his throat. he wants out. the cabin fever of being trapped beneath my human flesh has infuriated him. he wants to run, to sniff open air, to drink from the river and bathe himself in the waters.

but most of all, he seeks to devour. he does not care what or who. if it yields beneath tooth and claw, then the meat's origin is nothing he's concerned with.

the clouds part. the cold, shimmering face of mother moon rises in the west. she whispers to the wolf…

come out and play.

Leech

my crimson lake is becoming a dirty maroon now, but i'll float awhile longer. it's like my own personal spa, a chance to luxuriate and treat myself. if only i had two cucumber slices to place over my eyes. perhaps i should have cut slices from the cellulite-covered thighs of my college girls, that would have worked just as well. too late now. my blood meal is done with, and the tattered corpses now lie at the bottom of the lake, food for turtles and eels.

something feels suddenly strange. was it bad blood? no. the girls were pure and good. this sensation is in the mind, a twister of thoughts and images. i'm vaguely aware of my body sinking in the lake, my limbs twisting and contorting, a dark dancer in the depths.

the vision is more than welcoming. i see myself at the top of the skyscraper-house in Wyoming. a man-made waterfall rushes down onto me, my mouth wide and seeking, so eager for a taste. the waterfall is a combination of warm, exotic blood. humans. animals. every species of the earth blended into this delicious, potent cocktail, a nectar brewed in the veins of gods.

it's fucking orgasmic. i stare upwards towards the top of the waterfall and i see howling, tormented creatures there. angelic beings with faces full of love and light, their great white wings torn from their backs, their throats open only for me and pouring ever downward to slake my thirst.

the blood of angels.

i must hurry. the house draws me, and what a tasty house it shall be.

Apparition

i must try this experiment. something about it feels forbidden and wrong, but i'm helpless to deny the desire. she sits on a park bench in a trim business suit, chattering into her cell phone and occasionally jotting down notes on a legal pad. auburn hair, pale blue eyes, and features that appear both sharp and delicate.

i've decided to try with her.

i know it will be temporary. she may push me out immediately, but just a moment of flesh would be worth it. it feels like stealing, a bad thing, but really i am only borrowing her. i have no intention to stay. her body is her own, and to possess it forever would be a blasphemy.

she sees nothing of my fluttery cloud of a face. she does not feel my proximity to her, my spectral aura hanging about, longing for her skin, her pouting lips, and eyes that can look out on a world without fog or rain.

it will not be painful for her. invasive, yes, but i will not make it painful. she laughs into the cell phone, and i use this distraction to pour all of myself into her, snaky tendrils into her nostrils, ears, and cupid's bow mouth.

the cell phone falls into her lap. she sneezes just once, daintily. i can feel her thoughts, so confused, a cycle of fear and internal turmoil. i barely notice her background presence.

i am in her.

momentary flesh, and it feels divine.

Witch

we're just outside of Denver. it's as far as good ol' joe can take me. we part ways tomorrow, or so he thinks. he gave me a blanket and told me to curl up in the front, get a good night's sleep before starting out in the morning. that's what he's doing now. he's in his little sleeping alcove in the back, snoring loudly, a trucker's power nap.

i caress the blanket for a moment. sentimental joe. oblivious joe. i toss it down with the rest of the fast food trash beneath the seat. i lift myself up gracefully, following the unhealthy snuffling sound of joe's snores. slithering and half-crawling towards the sound, my movements serpentine.

i'm on top of him, the warm weight of me stirring him from his slumber. i'm unlatching his belt, his substantial beer gut fishbelly white beneath his shirt. he looks like a grubby old bear fresh out of hibernation, confused and groggy. i offer him my best smile, all red lips and smooth, dimpled cheeks.

his hand stops my wrist. his voice is meek, the voice of men as a whole. "my wife…"

it's weak, momentary resistance. if he really wanted to fight this he would have thrown me off him already. his jeans are around his ankles and i slide his pathetic stump between my thighs. it's like a cold root inside me, lumpy and unfulfilling. i ride hard, hips bucking, his flabby body flailing beneath me.

it takes him no time at all to reach orgasm. as his face contorts, i let my glamour slip…

Wolf

the beast is born in the rays of mother moon. he comes roaring out of the flesh, a ravager, claws black obsidian and teeth chewing to be free. his muzzle lifts, scenting the air. the chains jangle about his still morphing form. a small part of the man i am remains in the far back of his skull, but make no mistake, he's in charge now.

it's his wild world to devour and dominate.

he tests the chains, muscle against metal, so much power in this killing machine that is his body. he finds himself leashed. so much rage corrodes through his veins at the discovery of this. he shall not be tamed. he shall not be shackled. his is the gift of canines and incisors, and how he longs to bite and shred...

he lunges. the chain pulls taut against the birch trunk, bark falling downward. i will him to stop, a tiny voice within, but it's lost in the heavy breathing, his saliva splattering the dirt. another lunge, and a ragged crack forms in the trunk of the ancient birch.

he hunches his lupine shoulders, preparing for one last leap...and then the vision assaults his wolf mind. he's barreling across the plains. a gray house stands there, lording over the emptiness. the doorway swings open, and all that is inside is everlasting wilderness. rich loamy soil, plentiful game, and gigantic redwood trees. a predator's paradise. the sort of animal dream that makes the paws twitch with glee.

the beast sees himself there. running. hunting. killing. new territory. virgin land all his own.

Leech

the miles blaze by in the starlight. Texas is but a memory, a few food scraps still congealing in my lake of red. New Mexico was a blur of desert and asphalt. Colorado flies by now, the blue haze of the Rocky Mountains on the far horizon. the night steals the color from them, making them just distant blackened spikes in the windshield.

the top is down in the convertible, the crisp mountain air filling lungs that no longer require air. the mountains take me back into the corridors of my own mind, the twisted origins of life before unlife.

i'm there again in the rooms of memory, sitting in the psychologist's office. my legs are crossed as i sip my espresso. my suit alone costs more than every piece of furniture in this room. my hair is slicked back, immaculate, a golden blonde. skin flawless. smile sparkling.

it's easy to take care of yourself when you work on Wall Street earning fortunes by the minute. these sessions are supposed to be for grief counseling. a fellow co-worker and competitor met his untimely end recently. poor morton. brilliant, bespectacled morton. i gush about what he meant to me, how torn up inside i am about his passing.

truth be told, i baked him some delicious banana bread with a cyanide pill tucked away inside. bye bye, morton. gotta stay ahead of your competition!

she makes notes on her legal pad. i saw them afterwards. superficial charm. impaired empathy. bold egotism. scrawled notes like that…

Apparition

it's incredible. flesh returned, hands lifting up to touch and explore. i let her fingertips graze across her cheeks, her hair, and her perfect lips. it's like driving a motor car. i have to be aware of the right pedals and wheels to turn and push when i need to move her around.

she's still inside, her soul yelling out baffled entreaties. what is this? who are you? how are you inside of me? get out, get out, please get out!

i understand this is hard for her. she's panicking already, but i won't stay long. i'll spare her that, a mercy to this body on loan. it's the least i can do for the person that has reminded me exactly what real life tastes like.

the world around me is so fantastically colorful. the greens of the park, the blues of the polished fountain in the pond. oxygen tastes sweeter than ever before. the smells that are taken for granted, such wonderful, nostalgic aromas. a hot dog cart. wet leaves. my own temporary perfumed skin. i can have this again permanently if i reach the house. the thought is galvanizing. so much electric purpose behind it.

a man is approaching me. he recognizes the body, smiling with his briefcase in hand. he's handsome, hair a deep brown with just a little silver at the temples. she screams internally to him. help, jake! it's not me, jake! he cannot hear her. i don't respond either.

he's leaning inward for a kiss. i accept, tasting his salty lips. life…is everything.

Witch

he climaxes hard, his manhood twitching and spurting within me, and his gummy eyes open to gaze up at the temptress that seduced him into adultery. his eyes widen. he's awake now, fully awake. a low, horrified moan floats up out of his throat in the tight confines of the truck's cab.

he sees me as i really am, all glamour and bewitchment cast aside, the false youth peeled away. a wrinkled, withered woman sits atop his shriveling cock. he sees skin folded by time, sallow and dry, tits like drooping sacks. he sees a face sunken inward, a toothless grin greeting him, all purple gums and hard-hearted glee. my bald head shines in the dome light overhead, a few scraggly strands of white hair clinging to the liver spotted scalp.

i cackle into his face, loving the idiotic shock i see there. a stream of spittle oozes past my chin to stain his cheeks. my vulture's claw of a hand has already closed around the cold weight of the tire iron, and in one great blow, i bring it smashing down into his face. his teeth cave into his bleeding hole of a mouth. his nose splits. one of his eyes pops outward, nothing but nerve endings keeping it swinging from the socket.

i hit him again and again, pulverizing those stupid bloodhound features. soon his struggles stop and his body becomes still. he has no face now, just a gory soup of torn skin, warm blood, and brittle bone bits. i rip open his flannel and use the sharp end of the tire iron to begin carving the triangle symbol into his chest.

the old wiccan symbol for fire. fire...favor me.

Wolf

i come back to myself as dawn breaks. the chains are chill against my chest with morning dew clinging to the links. i'm vaguely aware of the events of the turn. it started bad, but it ended as it never has before. the wolf was charmed. he was cooed to like a newborn, and he curled himself into sleep beneath the birch. the house sent him pictures too, a mental lullaby for the animal inside.

what sort of power does this house possess? it must be unfathomable to soothe the beast that lives in me. it pulls both the man and the wolf, drawing us with personal promises. it recognizes the duality of who i am. it seems a worldly force, something that has an intimate understanding of all the dark, hidden things that live among men.

it calls to the monsters, flawed, brutal, and pitiful things that we are. it calls our names and we must answer. it only seems to want one thing from us. it wants to give, to release, to set things right…

but only after we show it our hearts.

what's in your heart?

i ask myself this. it's a riddle draped in mystique. bloodshed. ruin. innocent lives torn asunder. guilt. mountains of guilt. this is what is in my heart. these are the memories and moments that stain my ventricles, and the house wants to see.

it's show and tell for the house.

the house wants to see.

Leech

her face is burned forever into the realm of memory. i thought her a peculiar creature even then, someone not quite grounded in the ordinary ways of the world. pale moonflower of a face. sharp little chin. enormous gray eyes behind tortoise shell glasses and silver hair spun up into a tight bun. undeniably attractive, but almost too perfect with her long fingers and owl eyes. an agelessness about her. a beauty bordering on alien, her watchful frame mildly grotesque.

i remember the motivational poster in the frame behind her desk. the Rocky Mountains with the words "climb higher" scrawled beneath. my first psychologist. an inquisitive, ethereal entity with legal pad in hand. she was silent for a long time after i expressed all my counterfeit sorrow for morton.

"everything you've told me is a lie. the tears, a lie. the emotion, a lie. it's a human mask you wear, but underneath there is nothing but cruel curiosity. i've been searching for one like you. that's why i took this job…"

i didn't know how to respond. she's not supposed to speak to me this way. she's not supposed to see my soul like this. she folded her glasses and rose from the desk, standing in front of me, both regal and infinitely odd.

"you'll spend your lifetime being a cutthroat horror to all who cross your path. anything to advance your own interests. but then you'll die like all the rest of them die, and your bones will become dust. nothing grandiose about it. but if you had centuries…what would you become then?"

Apparition

i savor the kiss, making it last, the warmth of lips and the taste of love. i wish it could last forever, but i know it's my cue to exit. i leave her body just as our lips part, my essence filtering back out into the world of fog, the land of ghosts and the dead.

she collapses into his arms, weeping, and he holds her with a look of confusion on his face. she'll never understand what happened to her, and he'll never know either. just a little stolen moment, and then their lives will go on. they'll live, they'll love, and they'll pass on someday. i hope they appreciate all that they have before that day comes.

it's time to leave the cities behind. they're mesmerizing places, full of drama and humanity, but they also make me sad. i can watch life here, but that's all it'll ever be, just watching. a faceless face standing at a window covered in condensation and looking out while others raise families, chase dreams, and join hearts.

i'm an outsider here. just a breath of smoke in a world that lacks fire. no passion. no chance. my one chance lies in the Big Empty. that's where i'll find my fire. there's where i'll win the ability to make a kiss last without the use of another woman's lips.

i float on, the misty skyscrapers soon far behind me. no great buildings where i'm going. just miles of nothing, and in the center of all that nothing, a golden promise.

the best promise of all.

Witch

joe will never ride the lonely highways again.
joe will never hold his frail wife in his beefy
arms again. family man joe has become just
sacrificial meat for the pit lords. the
triangle is complete, a sigil of favor, all
carved flesh and dark, leaky blood.

may his wayward soul rot forever in the hell
circles, and may his stolen life be the lantern
to light my way through the Big Empty. this was
always his destiny. to play the victim. to die
alone and far from home.

i watch from the back of the truck's cab,
crouching downward and moving to open the
passenger side door of the big rig. for the
briefest of moments, i catch sight of my own
reflection in the truck's side mirror. my
glamour still cast aside, nothing but the real
me, the most honest version of myself presented
in all her gruesome glory.

i hate the sight that greets me. old, wrinkly
skin, sallow and decorated with moles. a
balding vulture-skull of a head, the hair just
little brittle sprigs, more of it falling out
with each passing day, hour, and minute. a
slimy hole of a mouth with eternally chapped
lips and not a single tooth left in my head.

so much ugliness. a roadmap of revulsion, this
face of mine, this body that traps me. my hands
lift up, just knobby red chicken claws in the
mirror, saturated in blood, the fingernails
long and curled inward.

i drive these balled fists into the mirror,
shattering it with a shriek building in the
back of my throat. no more ugly. no more crone.

Wolf

motorcycle days, motorcycle nights. starshine on my back and mountains on the horizon. open air for the lungs and scents to intoxicate the nostrils. the back roads hold endless stimuli for one such as me. when the wolf runs wild it's a curse upon the earth, but when the man has the wolf's senses, it's a gift that's indescribable.

the aromas of the land, my sense of smell heightened. the sights that come back to me from enhanced crystal clear vision. the feel of rattling handlebars in my grip and the intricate taste of the steak i ate earlier still lingering on my tongue. these are the things that make lycanthrope life worthwhile.

it's the beauty that sneaks up on the beast, the secret moments of the world that only animals can appreciate. i think of this as a great migration. i move with the birds, the mammals, and all the four-legged beasts that seek more plentiful pastures. a place to survive, a sanctuary to be free.

the house is my last chance.

my last migration across the backbone of America.

what will i find there?

i don't know. i can hope, but never truly know.

all i know for certain is that my journey ends there. it was always destined to end there. this curse, this life, this constant roaming…

all leading to this.

Leech

i've never been speechless, the gift of gab always mine to wield, silver tongue ready to lash against anyone and anything. but at that moment, in that dim office with her big, hypnotic owl eyes drinking in the secret side of my soul, i could think of absolutely nothing to say.

is this a madwoman that simply wears the suit of a psychologist? is she somehow connected to morton, a strange little waif with silver spidersilk hair and a petty lust for vengeance? how many seconds will it take me to grab up the vase on the table next to me and smash her skull open? what can i use to clean up the blood and brain when the deed is done?

these were the thoughts that burned through my head like a fever as she watched me. the most unsettling thing was that i got the distinct feeling that she heard these thoughts and found them amusing. what did she mean by centuries?

none of us can have centuries. impossible. all thing are fleeting. a fuck, a murder, a glass of good wine. none of those things last, and what a pity that is. i was about to open my mouth to ask her what sort of foolishness she was talking about, but that chance never arrived.

i remember her pouncing across the office like a panther and wrapping herself around me with the intimacy of a constrictor snake. i had the briefest second to feel the hardness of her flesh, almost like polished porcelain. and then the fangs found my throat, the blood gushed, and her lips suckled and teased at me.

i recall an inky state of rigamortis, vision blurry black, limbs twitching, a stiffening of organs and a hardening of bone. i could think of nothing but a boyhood memory, the time i killed a dove with a BB gun and let maggots strip the carcass clean in a shoebox over a period of weeks. that was how the turn felt for me. death came slow, taking its time, and maggots feasted on the parts that were still alive, making of me a private banquet.

sentience returned sometime later, hours or days, i cannot recall. i came back to myself as a mewling wretch, belly already burning with hunger, and you would think that this Victoria Frankenstein would stick around to dote over her creation, wouldn't you? perhaps a lesson or two about what she'd made me. guidance about the boon that had been so rudely forced into this newly dead flesh.

instead of her inquisitive face to greet me, i was born again into loneliness. her desk had been stripped clean, and even the walls were bare. it was like this had never been a psychologist's office at all, but just a trap waiting for the right victim to fall into it.

and so the experiment dragged himself up and spent days sucking down the blood of sewer rats and learning about his new state through nothing but trial and error. i never saw my maker again, she left no trail to follow, and perhaps that's the greatest insult. but if the house is all that it promises to be, perhaps i shall find my second deadbeat mother, and make her answer for what she did. the road is long, and the reveries flicker just like the headlights.

Apparition

it's so much quieter outside of the cities. i travel through the fields and the woods, floating over mossy stone walls and forgotten barbwire fences. i'm making good progress, and i glide faster than feet can ever walk.

sometimes i think i can hear the house whispering to me on the other side of the continent. words like "come, hurry, and be swift." it is excited to meet me, to invite me through the threshold and into a fine dress of new flesh.

i think only about the house now, nothing more. i allowed myself a distraction the night before. i came across another like me standing on the edge of an overgrown fire road. she was a poor, grisly wraith. a lady of the evening in life, her dress frilly and provocative. her ghostly countenance was decorated in knife wounds, not much face left except for hopeless wandering eyes.

she held her thumb out, a hitchhiker that will never be picked up again. i tried to speak to her. i implored her to see me, to interact with me, to share with me her thoughts. it was an exercise in futility. this one was too far gone, too long exposed to her own personal purgatory.

she remained in a loop, her own forever loop, and nothing would ever be able to reach her there. i felt sad. no purpose. no drive. no motivation to break out of a private hell and seek a new, undiscovered heaven.

i left her there with her thumb held outward. i am not like her. my purpose is clear.

Witch

Denver passed in a blur of indifference. joe's big burly self left an equally big mess, so i had to wash his remnants down a scummy bathroom drain before leaving that charnel house of an eighteen wheeler behind.

i'm near Casper now, Wyoming state line crossed many miles ago, and the call of the house has never been stronger. it vibrates in my ancient creaking bones, making a tuning fork of my skeleton. it says come old woman, come and see.

come and marvel at the wisdom in these walls. come and drink down magic from a well that runs so deep it touches the core of mother earth.

the path has been easy since the sacrifice of joe, and the pit lords have offered their protection in getting me closer to my goal. all perils fall to the wayside.

it's somewhere in the hidden valleys beneath the bighorn mountains. that is the place where the house pulses and beckons, a throbbing honey trap in an otherwise barren landscape. but there is honey there, that much i'm sure of. i'm familiar with hollow glamour, and the house is built from older stuff. more potent stuff.

whatever waits for me there is eldritch and poised, like calling to like, perhaps even a coven within the bowels of that great fortress. it's been many a decade since i've walked with a sisterhood of witches, but i'd gladly do it again for newfound power.

i'd do just about anything for that.

Wolf

Riverton to Thermopolis, Worland to Greybull, and each little hunk of Wyoming draws me closer. the bighorn mountains loom tall and blue on the horizon, and never have i faced more isolated country.

sometimes the sound of the choppy engine sends grouse bursting up from the sage, and the wolf within longs to give chase and rend the birds to feathered shreds. the grasslands appear vast, and it seems this place couldn't possibly harbor any great secret castle-cabins.

but my instincts know different. as soon as the road took me to Afton, i smelled the house across the lonely miles. it is a mix of aromas pleasing to both man and animal alike. for the man there is the stink of wood smoke, clear water, and acceptance. for the wolf the smell is more primitive. it is the stench of fresh meat, a new kill bled openly so that the iron scent drifts into the wind to be taken wherever it will.

there is compromise in the search for this strange place. rarely do the dual sides of me come to any kind of firm agreement. the wolf does what it will, and i am left to lament the rampages of an animal. but this is different.

for the first time since this curse fell like a fur-lined noose around my neck, i feel at peace with the idea of the beast that lives in my heart and my veins. perhaps he chases serenity too, but simply defines it in different terms.

we'll find the house. we'll sniff it out together...

Leech

the state trooper pulls in behind me when i'm still a few miles outside of Cody in the great state of Wyoming. he's all blaring sirens and angry flashers in his squad car, and oh how he hitches up that duty belt as he exits the vehicle and stomps his way towards the convertible.

i drum my fingers nonchalantly against the side of the car door while watching his approach in the rear view mirror. i was only doing 120mph. what's the harm in that? life is meant to be lived fast, especially if life is an endless tapestry stretched out before you.

he's all handlebar moustache and bluster when he reaches the window. he's a gruff shadowy face beneath a wide-brim hat, and for some reason he doesn't focus on the breakneck speed. he barks and points at the stop sign a few yards away that i "blew past".

"pardon the assumption officer, but i haven't seen another car out here in bumfuck nowhere aside from yours in about 98 miles or so. who exactly should i be stopping for? the fucking tumbleweeds?"

he doesn't like my tone. he's still barking and reaching for that iron on his hip as i exit the vehicle. i stroll over to the aforementioned stop sign and in one smooth pull i yank it from the dirt and wind it up like a baseball bat before smashing it directly into officer dipshit's blabbering face. the meat splits and the face explodes in a mushroom cloud of viscera. i lick warm blood off warm red metal.

officer dipshit is tasty, and i'm not stopping.

Apparition

it's not far. the living are forced to travel via flesh shells, but i have no such hindrances to hold me back. i am a light-footed shade passing through a dead world, and there is no traffic, no roadblocks, and nothing of the tangible to impede my progress.

all that holds me back is myself. it is the relic of my own mind that determines how fast or how slow i am to reach a premeditated destination. i may be a woman of want, but long have i languished in the isolation of a crumbling house full of misbegotten memories. a part of that reluctance stays with me. there are little whispers from the reeds that populate my thoughts, and each whisper seems obsessed with woe.

what will you find at the house? why go? why try? why move against a life tide that longs to consume you? i could just let go and become like that pitiful wisp with her hitchhiker's thumb extended for eternity. but something about giving up angers me.

i feel that i deserve more than the circumstances that have befallen me. the hand is poor, but the dealer is still shuffling, and there is a chance for something better. it might very well be the last hand that will ever be dealt to me.

will it be favorable? will i win through?

i'll never know unless i take the chance.

the gamble is all there is, and the game is nearing its end.

Witch

this is rough country, but no rougher than the creases and valleys that decorate my own face. each dry riverbed is like a familiar wrinkle, and the mountains are moles to be conquered in pursuit of lost vanity.

the terrain is a reminder of what i've become, and i resent it. the peaks i'm forced to cut through are rotting snaggleteeth, and each one seems to throb. the sun bakes overhead like a rheumy eyeball judging from the sky, and how i've hated that condemning eye in the looking glass reflection.

i wobble and weave across threadbare miles, and i see not another human soul, but i feel how incredibly close i am. the proximity awakens parts of me that have been desiccated and disused for longer than i'd care to admit. there's a wetness in that forgotten slit between my withered thighs, and i realize that i'm feeling arousal again.

a sensation so alien to me in my old age that i'd entirely forgotten what it feels like to desire something in the deep marrow of the bones. a desire to rule over and to make all else inconsequential.

i'm climbing the last craggy hill, and on some level i know that i'll see the house on the other side. it's patient, and it has been patiently waiting on me all this time.

the boards beckon.

the wetness spreads.

Wolf

howl. howl. howl. that is all that i want to do now. i want to throw back the head and unleash long mournful howls into the Wyoming night. i've ditched the bike, and i'm hoofing it across this final stretch. it's hard to maintain control when the house is this close.

the wolf wants to run, and with perked ears and gleaming fangs, he wants whatever the house has for us. visions flash like hot glimmers in the mind, and i see an unfurnished home that is nothing but the hive-house for a pack of slavering dogs. it stinks of canine, and draperies of torn meat hang from banister and windowsill. piss saturates the floorboards, and the marking of mutual territory is an art born of a yellow stream.

each room is a den to a bitch in heat, and the juices of those bitch hounds make the wolf brainsick and wild. more than usual. he wants to spill seed and lord over the forest internal. he wants pups, he wants a brood, he wants a legacy that will live on after his fur is gray and his claws are brittle.

i don't bother to leash him now. i let him push me beyond human limits on the trek. we cut through the base of a canyon, and the house lies to the west.

i don't know how i know this.

i just know.

and if i know...

the wolf knows.

Leech

i drove the convertible through the sagebrush until the tires popped like overripe grapes, and then i left the dearly departed titty dancer's slutmobile to fade into a colorless heap of metal under the blaze of Wyoming stars.

i had resigned myself to walk, but wouldn't you know it, fate just favored me with another big ol' toothy grin. the herd of wild horses watched me from beneath a few scraggly cratageus trees. a few lively ponies, a mare, and one bold stallion with the silkiest chestnut coat. i willed the stallion and the mare closer with a glamour gaze, and i clapped my hands with gunshot after gunshot to send the ponies fleeing.

they watched me helplessly with rolling eyes, wanting to run, but locked in place with my oh so commanding stare. i took pleasure in taking a thumbnail to the mare's throat and opening it up, and what a faucet she was, a great heap of knobby legs and sleek horseflesh that finally collapsed down into a puddle of her own unexpected death. i made the stallion watch, and in his suffering i obtained submission.

now he's my mount, and i'm driving him like the devil's own across the hilly desolation. i whip him ceaselessly with a length of cratageus limb, and the thorns have shredded his flanks to the point where his ribs are visible. after each lash i lick the whip, and that sweet equine plasma makes me swoon as we gallop.

he grinds his teeth, frothing at the mouth and nostrils, and finally his legs give out when we're near the house. shame, but i could use the energy. every weary traveler needs a drink.

Apparition

the mist parts, and the house is there. foggy tendrils caress the black boards, and the carved oaken door is akin to a mouth bearing a warm and welcoming smile. its scale is hard to fully comprehend. there are peaks and arches, basalt columns supporting the weight of the wood, and windows aplenty, each one a glimmering orb that betrays nothing of what is concealed within.

the house is a puzzle, a jigsaw missing pieces that only i can provide, and i am eager to make it whole. that's not quite right. perhaps i am the puzzle with the missing pieces. i am the one that needs to be made whole again.

i feel no trepidation at the sight of the house. the unspoken invitation is clear, and i am floating with an unseen breeze. it's like a light wind tunnel pulling me closer to that threshold, and i am all too willing to go.

there is nothing surrounding the house. it sits on a patch of land that is barren of growth and vegetation. there is only soil to support the foundation, and the feathered bits of fog lift up from the ground to tease and play at the windows.

the door and i come together, and i pass through a barrier of wood like water through an aquarium filter. i'm assaulted by the vibrancy of the interior. no mist, no colorless environment, but a place that is flushed with comfortable life. i almost think that i hear a mastodon-sized heart beating from somewhere in the bowels, and this alone fascinates me.

the house is alive. more alive than me…

Witch

it is painted of the darkest dark i've ever laid my poor old peepers on. it is obsidian, it is onyx, it is oil in an ancient engine, tar in a deep pit, night plastered across moonless night, and not a single star in the house's blissful sight. i fall instantly in love, a schoolgirl again, and the crush nearly shatters me.

the turrets and spires twist up into the sky, and the great wrought gate beckons. it stinks of promises. books of power, scrolls of worth, cauldrons with thick rims and incantations the likes of which i've never experienced before.

i am made spineless with wonder. i creep forward, a humbled thing, and a part of me thinks black lightning will blast from those window-eyes and strike me down, burn me up to cinders, and salt the earth with the ash of one of the last true witches of the world.

the shadows of sayres dance from behind stained glass, and horny goats postulate and prance from side to side. naked women of the woods writhe somewhere inside, all of them made drunk on the blaze of infernal bonfires. nubile, fresh, clean, and born anew into fine flesh. gifts of the house, and gifts soon to be mine.

i hobble gleefully across a moat of pitch black boards, and from the sour water below baby mandrakes giggle and reach for me. their deformed root faces twist and twitch, all of them waving pitiful limbs at the gaping aperture leading inside.

i'm here. finally here.

Wolf

it's an island in a sea of towering pines, and the logs that comprise the structure must have been dragged across bleak valleys by the shoulders of giants. woodsmoke curls up from chimney after chimney, and soon all is lost in that aroma. it's the scent of a home.

it is like that mythical hall where odin and his kin drink ale and tell tales of glorious war until raganarok comes. it's a place for a tired man to rest, and even shaggy fenrir can stretch out in front of the fireplace to let it dry the blood on a snout that is forever wet.

i see a cabin of colossal scope, but the wolf sees more. for him, it's a forest without decisive end. no boundaries, no place where the foliage stops, but just nature unbound and trees of the most primordial sort. deer, rabbits, moose, bear, and all the critters of the animal kingdom prowling, seeking mastery from an alpha king.

i do not hike anymore. i run, and the wolf runs with me.

we run like this is a mirage, an illusion that could flicker out at any second, and we pound our shared feet across the hardpan to reach the house before all those lanterns in the windows burn out.

i'm slavering, the saliva dripping down my chin, and i have absolutely no desire to reach up and wipe it away. let it flow. let it be.

the wolf and i feel rare kinship as we leap through the door.

Leech

the stallion blood still sloshes in my gut, and when the house comes into view, i think for a moment that it's plasma intoxication. it's too glorious to be real. too fantastical to be a tangible place. it's just so fucking perfect...

it's a blazing black like what's left after decades of an underground coal fire, but little bursts of red snake up from the boards. the red comes from blooming roses, the petals thick and sensuous, and each one drips with a special scarlet nectar. it's ludicrous, but the roses bleed. they bleed for my benefit. they pour and stream with delicate droplets of pink slime, and i want to wrap my lips on those petals and suck until my throat numbs.

the house itself is a phenomenal conundrum. it has traditional siding, but the height is staggering, a gargantuan skyscraping tower that seems to spear the clouds above. each plate window gleams with maroon strobe lights, and the silhouettes of curvaceous women frolic and cavort on multiple floors.

this house nurtures the worst parts of me. the urges, the desires, and the tendencies to do harm purely for the sake of how thrilling it is. i want to swallow, i want to gorge, i want to lick down lakes of blood. i want to feast on entire generations, and if the eldritch core of this house comes into my possession, i think it wholly possible that i can slurp down the lives of every living entity in the entire known universe.

arrogant of me? no. just ambitious.

and ambition draws me in.

Apparition

the foyer is huge, the ceiling like a domed cathedral. an ornate spiral staircase dominates as the centerpiece of the room, and i marvel at the lit candles that line the banisters. i feel so present in the house, and that is a sensation that i haven't felt for a long time.

a man stands behind me. i become dimly aware of his presence, but i'm confused about where he could have come from. he was not there before. there was nothing but a wall of black lacquered wood, and now there stands a gentleman in an equally black tailed tuxedo.

something about him is not quite right. he stands totally still, and he is more of a caricature of a human, something masquerading as traditional flesh and blood. he is bald, and his facial features are almost impossibly compact. eyes close together, mouth a small cupid's bow, and nose nothing but a nub on a mound of pale pinkish skin.

the eyes are the most surreal. they are just little black pits, pupils almost indescribable. they resemble doll eyes to me. just little glossy button doll eyes.

that is not what shocks me. that is not what freezes me in place, a whirling figure of ectoplasm and confoundedness. it is how the man in the tux is looking at me.

he is not looking through me like all others do.

he is staring directly at me, and his eyes seem to cleave to the center of the soul.

Witch

i did not expect to be greeted. i expected the freedom to explore the house at whim. but i have been approached by a man who seems to have just detached himself from the very wall. i'm in a circular library with book stacks that circle for what looks like forever, and altars with miscellaneous ingredients are placed sporadically for my viewing pleasure.

there must be magic in the man. not a warlock, but something else. he is infinitely strange to behold. his eyes are just little drops of oil beset in a gaunt skull, and his features look like they've been mashed in with a blunt hammer.

he speaks, and it is a voice filled with flat charm.

"welcome. the house calls, and you came."

"is the house yours?"

he smiles. his teeth are tiny, almost like an infant's first set.

"not hardly. i hold no such honor. consider me a steward for a force much greater than myself. an emissary for the house, and a mouthpiece in times of necessity. a fragmented proxy to what and where you are."

"and what is this place? what spells brought it into being?"

"always thinking of magic. devoted to your craft. seeker of knowledge, hunter of youth. think of this as a house of judgment. a place where the witch trials are not born of fearful superstition, but much more honest…"

Wolf

he calls himself the host. i thought if anyone was here it would be some grizzled mountain man with a tangled beard, but i'm seeing fancy instead of rustic. i get no real feeling from the man. he doesn't seem bad or good, wrong or right, straight or crooked.

the wolf tries to take in his scent, but the host smells of nothing. he is ephemeral, and maybe that's how he wants to present himself.

i marvel at the lofts, the fireplaces, the walls decorated in mounted deer heads and yarn-stitched dreamcatchers. it's like the grandfather of all cabins in the house, and it just goes on and on. the host moves to one of the fireplaces, and i follow him, warming my palms in front of the blaze.

he clasps his hands, miniscule hands that look odd hanging from such large sleeves, and he turns his own carbon-colored eyes to the fire.

"this house is special. it draws the ones such as you. outcasts, pariahs, angels to some, demons to many, beasts of the field and corpses of the night. things unspeakable, and things considered mere fables. but we know better, don't we? monsters are real. i know because i'm talking to one."

i don't know what to make of the host. where is he going with this? what does it all mean?

"why all the trouble? i'm nobody these days."

"you're somebody here. everyone is somebody in the house. it'll help you figure out for yourself who that somebody is."

Leech

he leads me past chambers of fleshy delights. there is corrupted carnality all around me, and each dead pore feels utterly stimulated. my preternatural eyes shine with bottomless lust, and i imagine fucking and clawing my way through every room. i realize on some level that's brainsick behavior. it's no better than an addict after a needle.

i don't care though. i want what i want, and i'm comfortable with taking.

"everything you see here is a reflection. it represents your moral complexity, or lack thereof. you see bodies you want to possess. you see rivers of blood, and you want to drink each of them dry. you see an environment to control and subjugate. it is what you are. the self-serving, amoral being that you've become."

i throw a cool sideways glance at the man in the tux. the host, as he so politely introduced himself upon my entrance. he doesn't look like much to me. a puppet in sleek threads. i sense that he's bloodless. nothing worth drinking, and nothing worth savoring. he's hollow like a babooshka doll, and i don't think it'll take much to rip him open when i tire of his little tour.

"digging around in my head, are we, friend?"

"not me. the house. it sees you. it sees your heart. all of your heart. every debauched and stained inch. how do you feel about that?"

i shrug.

"always been a bit of an exhibitionist."

Apparition

"you see me? you really do?"

"i see parts of you that you don't even see anymore. buried parts. lost parts. the parts we hide to get along. a ghost, a shade, a monster…they're not so different from a person. every human is layered. decisions define them, and decisions define monsters too."

"did i make the right decision coming here?"

"that depends on what you want from the visit."

"what do you mean?"

"you crave something that was taken. a body that is gone. a life that was already lived. a road that you've already walked intimately before."

"is that so wrong? don't i deserve a second chance? i'm lonely. i'm tired. my memories are like an old book of photographs. pages are missing. faces are half-formed. i've lost so much already…"

"there's a reason you linger. you have to confront that reason. you can do it here, and be free. or you can chase a chance at another body. it's your choice. everything before and after this will be your choice."

"why can't i remember?"

"try harder. the house will help."

Witch

"for you, it's always been about fear. you're afraid of dying. you're scared of your own face, and the ugliness that you think you see. you'd steal youth rather than face that. you'd sacrifice innocents to make your own sagging skin just a little more supple. it's time to let go of that. fear makes cowards of us all, and cowards hate needlessly."

i find myself hating the host. he'd paint me as a sniveling wretch. i've wreaked havoc in my day. i've called up demon kings and made entire fields of crops blacken with spite.

"so what is the house? just a glamour? a paltry imitation of power? that's no use to me. i'll not be judged for what i had to do to get by. you don't understand what it's like to be maligned."

"the house understands. those are justifications and excuses, but in the end you have to be honest with yourself. you've hurt others because you carry hurt in yourself. still time to change. still time to be better than what your detractors think you are."

for the briefest moment something like hope shines through, but i stomp it down in my mind and sweep it beneath a dirty mound of straw. i feel cheated. drawn across hundreds of miles to be dressed down.

i fork my fingers at the host, and i start to spit out the most destructive curses that i've ever learned.

Wolf

"do you often think of the people you've killed?"

the question stings. i don't want to talk about it, but i might as well be truthful. i've kept it all locked up during my isolation. no one to confide in. no one to confess to…

"every day. i wonder about what lives they might have led. i wonder about the families that were left behind. i wonder about the families that never even got started because of me. daughters never mothered. sons never fathered. just these blank patches in the lives of my victims, and nothing can ever fill those holes up again. i'm responsible for those holes. so many personal paths ruined because of the bloodlust of a single instant."

i feel salty wetness in my eyes. i blink it away. i'm undeserving of the tears. let those tears be for the ones that lost their loved ones.

"wish i could undo it. take it all back. should have put a silver round into my skull back when it all started."

"guilt is natural. guilt is human. that pain in your heart is good. doesn't feel good, but it is. it reminds you that you did terrible things when you weren't yourself, and you're sorry for it. you must understand that an animal makes no conscious decision to be evil or cruel. a predator is just what nature made it. it distinguishes not between the meat of a deer or a person. it hunts and it eats only to survive. you can't tame a wild beast, but you can learn to stop it from doing a certain kind of harm."

Leech

the host tells me about all the damage i've caused. he spins these grandiose stories about the negative effect my actions have had on the world. it's like he wants me to drop to my knees here in the house and beg for atonement.

i'm trying so damn hard to suppress laughter. moans of mingled anguish and pleasure serenade us, and i let my fingertips drift past silky curtains to brush against ripe and willing forms. the host is a bore. and i find it ever so hard to stomach the mundane.

"she gave you immortality, but that didn't change you. you are what you have always been. you were a monster even before you were turned. that's your creed. your legacy. are you satisfied with it?"

"enough with the compliments, fancypants. i'm starting to blush. as much as i'm enjoying this little heart to heart, i'm much more interested in eating a few hearts. care to show me a menu?"

"nothing here is edible for one such as you. as i've told you, it's all just mental projection. the house is what you make of it."

i start to fume a bit on the inside. nothing edible? nothing that actually bleeds? so it's all just tricksie bullshit?

"i'd call that false advertising. and truth be told, your creepy butler routine is starting to piss me off."

"when i get angry…i get thirsty."

Apparition

he says to remember. he says to search deep. the house clears the fog, and a well of uncertain memories lies beneath. do i dare dip into that well? what if i don't like what i find?

"even the dead can repress things. especially if it's the worst kind of thing. something worth burying and hiding. there's a secret in you, but it's gone quite dark, and to light it up again without warning can be dangerous. take it slow. don't let it consume you."

"the secret has always been there, but it's how you react to it that matters."

"why are you still here? why do you linger? what holds you back? find those answers. look into the heart that you once had. what did it harbor when it used to beat? what emotions predominated?"

the words are like a flood, and i cannot hold it any longer. the dam is breaking. the images are coming. i don't want them. i want to leave. this house was a mistake. coming here…a mistake.

i see that little boy and that little girl. i see them in the old home that once imprisoned me. i see a man too, a regal man with fluffy sideburns. i see myself kissing the man. i see myself holding the children, teaching them, reading to them, loving them, and cooking for them in a sunlit kitchen.

i see the husband i used to have. the son and daughter that were both mine. the family that was once my own.

Witch

the curses make impact. the words are vile, and they spew from my mouth in a torrent. in normal cases such curses take immediate effect. they rot a person out. they cause the late stages of consumption. they drive sane men mad and force women to throw themselves from cliffs.

they hit the host full force, all of these dirty banes of mine, and what happens?

they do nothing but rock him like a light breeze. he does not rot, because he has no true flesh. he does not bleed out, because his veins lack plasma. he does not become a lunatic because the corridors of his brain are incomprehensible, not comparable to that of a typical human.

he is immune to magic. he soaks it in with absolutely no expression on his face except for mild disappointment. i take in a breath to try again, but it's too late. the house sucks me backwards like a vacuum, and soon i'm falling through some narrow trapdoor. i land with a crash, and i rise up to survey my new surroundings.

i am naked, stripped of all rags and cloths, and if that is not enough, the glamour of false youth has been taken too. i am nothing but my pitiful self down here. no power. no arcane gifts.

just a cowardly old woman boxed in on all sides by towering funhouse mirrors.

Wolf

"you're a man with a rare problem. a carnivore lives inside of you. a rampaging carnivore that is governed only by how frequently it can track and dispatch prey. you are forever blended to the life of this carnivore. if it is wounded, you are wounded. if it starves, you starve. that's a bond with incredible depth, but the two of you don't fully know each other yet."

"the house would like to offer you both a chance to connect with each other."

"that might be a bad idea."

i don't know exactly what the host is offering, but i've seen what happens when the wolf comes out. there's no talking with him. no communication. he gets his point across with the gnashing of serrated teeth.

"i know the concept troubles you, but fret not. he'll be docile here. he knows it is safe place, and he is not backed into a corner. this is as much a sanctuary for the wolf as it is for you. open your hearts. explore them together, man and animal intertwined."

"many are resistant. so many monsters come to this house, and so many of them are too stubborn or too violent to garner the benefits of such a place. you have the potential to be different. redemption is a process, and this is the first step."

"take it. take it with both foot and paw…"

Leech

"*so here's the deal, host with the most. i came here with high hopes. i'm looking to get fed, but so far all you're feeding me are empty promises. that's a problem.*"

"*you have glutted yourself for too long already. the house can teach you to abstain. it can show you a better way.*"

"*just what the fuck is this place? i'm not looking for a rehab clinic.*"

"*a complicated question calls for a complicated answer. the house is different for each individual. it's paradise to some. it's a warm home or a familiar place. for others it can be a prison. a cathedral of temptation. a graveyard for monsters. you make of it what you will. monastery or mortuary. that choice is yours.*"

i find myself stalking the host now. he's walking backwards at a clipped pace, and each room we pass seems to rebel against my presence. those nubile limbs go from beckoning to aggressive. they grip at me, reaching and tearing at my clothes, and i smash down on them with hammer blows, the vampiric strength shattering bone and lacerating flesh with ease.

"*celibacy isn't my thing, and i'm not much of a church-goer. a mortuary it is then. any preference on where i place your body once i separate that little bald head from your shoulders?*"

"*this is a mistake for you.*"

"*nah. but inviting me in? that was a mistake.*"

Apparition

a boy, a girl, a husband, and me the happy homemaking wife of the once proud plantation mansion. it was perfect. on the surface it was so completely pure, a flawless family, all smiles and happiness. but nothing is always what it seems.

sometimes things squirm under the surface.

things squirmed in me that blazing summer. paranoid thoughts and feelings of inadequacy. i saw how he'd been looking at the maids. spending late nights in his study and not coming to bed until long after midnight. i thought he didn't want me anymore. i thought he found me repulsive. a marriage of convenience is a bloated covenant, and soon it started to seep with decay.

but if i left, what would befall the children? those little sweetlings. all that i had. all that i loved. i would be parted from them, and the sorrow would eat through whatever would be left of me by then.

my suspicions were confirmed when i took the lantern to the barn and found him with his trousers around his ankles, plowing not the field, but the pretty mulatto that served our dinner and washed our soiled linens.

heartsick pain. anguish of the most intense sort. rage, rage, rage, and nowhere to put it. the nervous breakdown followed, and with it came actions i cannot be responsible for.

someone else must have committed them. i was not there. i was out of my head. a prim housewife is surely not capable of savagery…

Witch

i look at what i am. wasted breasts that hang like deflated balloons, skin rubbery and befouled, the blubber rolls like worms, and hands and feet just tiny crab claws balled up into inexpressible distress.

the mirrors are everywhere, and they show me versions of myself that are fat, elongated, crooked, bent, malformed, and worse even than the true reflection. i have been screaming since i got here. beating at the mirrors and leaving smeared red handprints across them.

the glass doesn't break and the glass doesn't lie.

the glass is just for me.

it all comes roaring back. farmers i've cursed for their success. fair maidens i wrongfully bewitched because i was jealous of their beauty. animals i opened up in service of the uncaring pit lords. twisting myself, corrupting myself, damning myself in the most self-destructive ways.

the strength slinks away, and i fall to my knees with a meaty plop. thoughts are fading. knowledge is becoming pointless. the mirrors show a gibbering, drooling idiot, a woman of untold dementia who shits her adult diaper and sits in her own urine puddles.

a sense of catatonia comes.

i am afraid to fight it, afraid of losing what is lost already, and so i welcome it.

Wolf

i don't know how it's possible, but the house has shrunk down to an intimate black room with low orange light emanating from the walls. it messes with my spacial awareness, and i see that i'm sitting in a leather chair on some raised platform. the host stands beside me with his arms crossed, but i barely notice him.

i'm looking across the room at the platform opposite to mine. there sits a huge timberwolf with sable fur and yellow globe eyes. he watches me with caution, his ears perked and his attention rapt.

i watch him right back.

"this is the carnivore inside of you. the animal that you share your body with. the big bad wolf that has taken bite after bite out of any opportunity you've ever had to lead a normal life. i know you resent him for that, but try not to. think of this not as a confrontation, but as a formal introduction."

i lift up a little in my chair, and the wolf growls low in his throat, those glistening white fangs becoming visible as the purple lips pull back from the teeth. the jaw unhinges, and he snaps his teeth together a few times, the clacking sound echoing through the room.

"he's as wary of you as you are of him. being what you are is unnatural for both. he wants one thing, and you want another. you want the life of a man. he wants the life of a wolf."

"time to compromise."

Leech

"threatening me doesn't help you. the house won't like it."

"i really don't care what the house likes or doesn't like. if this place is just a façade, then it's no good to me, mr. host. i'm lured here and then treated like a child?"

the walls are rippling all around me. some deep noise emanates from the depths of the house, and it's like the bellow of a leviathan-sized beast.

the walls become transparent, and images of my own face are plastered across them. the face moves with various expressions of raw emotion, but the most prevalent one is a rictus of hate.

"you're trying to play me. and when you play me, you're just begging for me to open you up and start playing with parts of you."

the host continues to retreat, and the hallways of the house seem to narrow as we go. there seems to be no dimensional law at place here, and solid surfaces are as fluid as liquid. it's jarring, but it won't distract me from getting to him. the house might be a weird cipher, but if i torture the host and make him squeal enough, i figure i'll get some answers about what fuels this place. every power source has some kind of fuel. i don't know what it is, but i know that i want it.

something stops me. an intuition that offends all of my senses.

"is there a fucking hound here? a moon dog? this corridor stinks of wolf…"

Apparition

i wasn't myself when i took up that pitchfork and drove it through my husband's torso while he was still thrusting into her. the rusty tongs impaled them both, and they writhed together like dying slugs. i nailed them to the floor. they died messy. they died like bugs dripping with internal juices.

i don't know how that happened. i don't know why i did that. i was upset. i was betrayed. marriage is sacred, isn't it? you shouldn't put your wife through such a trauma. he was a dirty cheater, and i had to avenge my own pride.

i sobbed into the straw for awhile after it was done. i traced lazy spirals in the blood that pooled on the barn floor. i knew instantly what i had to do. no son or daughter should be without a father. i didn't want to subject them to a broken home. they didn't need to be made victims of my shame and my sadness.

and so i smothered little sally in her bed with a goosefeather pillow. it was quick. she looked flushed and happy when she stopped breathing. it was harder with michah. i woke him in the night to bathe him, and he knew something was wrong. he knew something was wrong even as i drowned him in the tub with bubbles lifting from those little boy lungs. poor sweetlings. i was put in an awkward position. it was for the best.

nothing was done out of malice. i did that for them. i saved them from an unjust world full of liars and slicksters.

and they wouldn't be alone. of course i intended to follow.

Wolf

a rough pink tongue lolls out to lick at a grizzled muzzle. the eyes watch me cautiously, but without malice. i've always thought of the wolf within as a hideous aberration, something monstrous that has the ability to repulse and horrify. but up close like this, i realize that the wolf is eerily beautiful. he is nature embodied in the rawest form, and the sleekness of his coat smells of fir and pine. there's feeling in the eyes of the wolf. a worried animal. he looks as scared of me as i've always been of him.

our eyes lock, and i approach him. his growl intensifies, but he holds his ground, clawed paws digging into the platform. i try to make it clear that i'm not aiming to do him harm. i just want to get close. i want to reach out and touch the part of me that is wild and uncontrollable.

it is here in the flesh for the first time since this nightmare began, and i feel that i'll never get this chance again.

i must confront what i am. i can't hide it anymore. i can't sweep it away with isolation or lock it up with chains. it's inhumane to do that, and looking at this animal now, i see that it is as lost and confused as me. it doesn't understand why it shares its body with a human. it is as cursed with this unnatural symmetry as i am.

i let my hand reach out, fingertips limp and questing. i take up the most non-threatening stance i possibly can. the wolf's ears flatten across that bullet-shaped skull, but he does not launch himself at me. that is a start.

Leech

"you don't understand the intricacies of the house. i am not one, but many. i am a host to all of the monsters that hear the call and respond to the invite. there are other versions of me here. each room has a host, and each hallway has a variation of me. there are other visitors too. for once in your life, it's not all about you. i know you're unaccustomed to that."

"sounds like you're stalling. or even better, sounds you're trying to serve me a steaming plate of bullshit. bullshit gives me indigestion. it also offends me. i could care less if you have yourself a wittle pet moon dog somewhere in this hellhole. i'm not concerned with that. i want you to take me to whatever keeps this house afloat. i want the source, mr. host."

"you be a good host and do me that honor, and i won't pull your leg clear from your body and use your femur as a straw to drink down whatever nastiness it is that keeps you sentient."

i'm on him now, and i thrust my hands into the silky material of the host's tux. i swing him around by the collar, and he moves like a weightless thing, just a dead leaf whirling with the wind. i pop the fangs and i get in real close, inhaling deeply of this thin-skinned steward. he smells of sterile nothingness.

"i cannot do what you ask. it is beyond me, and attempting to menace something as eldritch as the house is beyond you too."

Apparition

i have been tricked. this house is gaslighting me, and i will not stand for it. it is unearthing ugly things, ugly memories, and i want them to go away again. i deserve my second chance. i can do better. everyone makes mistakes.

once i have flesh all my own again, a body with blood and breath and a womb, i will find a new husband, i will make wonderful new children, and i will start again. i can make it right. i can have another family. a better family.

but i need a body. and even if i must jump from one to the next until i find the perfect match, then i will do it. i feel hot even as a spirit, a rushing wave of furious spectral malevolence. i want out of here. i want to walk on living legs out of here.

i hurl myself at the host, seeking to enter him in the way that i entered the woman in the city. i delve through his pores and into his mouth and nostrils, but it's instant vertigo, he's dark inside, hollow inside, and dust bunnies float in the empty chamber where his organs should be. just as soon as i'm in him, i feel repelled. he blasts me back out of him with some psychic push, and i'm tumbling downward into a room full of mirrors.

there is an old naked crone kneeling down here. she is catatonic with drool dripping down her chin. she's not ideal, but she'll do.

i want a body. i want out.

and with these thoughts circling, i invade the woman's decrepit old bones.

Wolf

my fingertips want to start trembling, but i let the composure take hold, and i utilize my will to keep my hand steady. the wolf watches, and some of the mistrust starts to fade. his wide nostrils flare, and he takes in my scent. it doesn't threaten him. it isn't the scent of a rival. he smells himself, and this confuses him.

it makes him aware that he is a member of a pack, a pack of two, and this is the first time the pack-mates have had a chance to openly communicate. his snout inches closer, and a tentative tongue slips past the gate of his serrated teeth. i feel the wetness of his hot saliva as he licks me, and something in me changes.

i've always seen this thing as the enemy. a horrible scar on my life, and a burden on my soul. i don't see that now. i see an animal that doesn't know any better. i'm not looking into the eyes of something that is malicious. dark and primal? yes, but that is just how mother nature made him. he has his flaws just like i have mine.

i push my luck and i place my hand across his head, allowing my fingertips to brush against that bristly fur. he resigns himself to be stroked. he does not bite or growl, and it's clear this is a bold gesture on his part. he is a beast of the wild, and to show even the most miniscule submissive side goes against his genetic makeup.

we bond in the house. we bond right before everything goes to hell.

Leech

i mull over the idea of working over the host a bit more until he starts becoming more cooperative. it's clear he's pretty tightlipped, though. that's probably why i forgo any additional discussion and snap my head forward to lock onto his jugular. i chew and i chew, masticating on his formless flesh, and a fetid black ooze flows from the wound.

it isn't blood, and it has no warm consistency to it. it tastes like black licorice mixed with old motor oil. i spit up most of it and just keep gnawing, but a little of it manages to seep down the back of my throat.

usually when i'm tasting a sloshing meat-sack i have a fun little sensory experience. i get flashing images of the person's past, future, and even fragments of their dreams. nothing comes from the host but images of the house. forlorn hallways, corridors to nowhere, and doors that open into vast starless places.

he tastes like one bad penny, and i don't much care for the flavor. he feels like he's crumpling in on himself, just fragile bones in a tux. i snarl and throw him into the wall, and strangely enough, it shatters inward like darkened glass.

he lands in a heap, punctured and crawling, and i stomp in after him. i lift my head, and what a sight i see. seems we crashed another of the house's quirky little parties.

there's another host, identical to the first.

there's also a man…and a wolf.

Apparition

there is no opposition from the old woman. she's a dim bulb that has chosen to burn out, and when my essence floods through her, i am instantly in charge of new flesh. it's withered and creaky, like entering a poorly maintained building that is fit to crumble, but body beggars can't be body choosers.

i make her stand up and i race to the closet mirror, balling up her fists and using her arthritic knuckles to beat and bash against the glass. it smashes after enough violence, and i hold the bloody hands close to her sagging abdomen.

i stagger the meat vehicle through the threshold, and we come to a white door. the knob is polished silver, and it is decorated with little carved stars. maybe it's the exit. maybe it's the way out of the house. i am eager to leave. i am eager to get this shambling old flesh full of seed so that it can usher in new life. i will use every bit of my ghostly essence to make sure the baby is healthy and alive even if it kills the vessel. i can always find a new body to mother it with.

i take the knob and i push the door inward, and i realize my mistake far too late. the body i inhabit is sucked out into deep space, the frigid pressure biting into brittle bones. we float, but by some blasted magic from the house, we are allowed to breathe. there is nothing out here but distant stars and absolute silence.

the door closes behind us, and it is like it was never there. i have the flesh i wanted. i have the life i craved. i am perfectly alone with it, and my screams go unheard in the void.

Wolf

he is a bat out of hell, a gaunt grinner with black organic matter smeared all over his mouth. i have heard about the dead ones, the ones that still walk by consuming the blood of the living, but i have never encountered one before. i always knew in the pit of my stomach that they were out there, but i never thought i'd see one in my travels.

this one looks mad. his eyes shine with terrible mirth, and as the wounded host crawls across the floor, the vampyre strides forward and curb stomps the back of his head. it explodes like a rotting pumpkin, and chunks of that dark slime splatter all over the room.

the dead one leans back on his heels and inhales deeply before shaking his head from side to side.

"knew i smelled dog. so what's this? the house has its own little kennel for slavering moon mutts? what's that make you? his fucking keeper?"

i rise up to my feet, and i find that my hands have balled into fists at my sides. the wolf is calmly stepping from the platform, his claws clicking against the marble floor. we are both defensive. we both know this leech means harm to us, and for the first time in forever, the wolf and i are fully on the same page.

"it's a little more complicated than that."

"huh. cute lil pup, isn't he? one question."

"does he bleed?"

Leech

i turn my attention away from the man and the wolf for a moment as the second host approaches. he seems almost to mourn his fallen copy, and then he moves to within a few inches of me.

"your heart is flooded with bad blood. nothing can be done for you here. you are a lost cause, and even the house pities one as faithless as—"

he's about to finish his thought, but his babbling irritates me, so i reach up and take his soft little baby head in my hands and spin it on the neck, relishing that dry crack as whatever serves as his vertebrae snaps. he falls in a boneless heap, and i step over him, once more turning my attention to the odd pair standing before me.

they both smell of moon dog. i sense that the changeling blood is in both of them, but i've never seen ones like this. moon dogs are usually this wretched patchwork of human flesh and wolf flesh. they're thoughtless, blundering beasts that deserve nothing but an ugly death.

these two are almost like both parts separated from each other. i find that interesting.

"you won't touch him."

"won't i?"

i could keep on trading words, but i've had about all i can stomach of this house. i'll murder this moon dog and wreck the place before i go. it's the least i can do after receiving such a gracious and disappointing invitation.

Wolf

the leech makes his move, and his fist barrels into my gut with the force of an iron piston connecting with flesh. all of the air whooshes from my body, and i crumple backwards while holding both hands against my abdomen. i wasn't ready for that. his limbs are impossibly hard, and he comes for me again, sending several knees into my torso to subdue me. each hit rattles my skeleton and makes my teeth chatter.

his strength is otherworldly, and i am outmatched against this reanimated dead man. he grips me by the throat and prepares to send a headbutt into my face, and i fear that such a hit will make my entire nose explode into a blooming red crater. he never connects.

the wolf strikes first.

the beast is a flash of fangs, and all those serrated edges sink deeply into the vampyre's calf muscle. the meat is hardened deadflesh, but the teeth of such a wolf are potent, and they lodge deep as he shakes his muzzle from side to side. the leech snarls with pain, and he uses his other leg to boot the wolf in the side of the head with all of his might.

the blow is brutal, knocking the wolf clear and sending him tumbling over his own four legs halfway across the room. he whines in the back of his throat, but it doesn't take him long to shake it off and leap back up to his feet. the leech is about to intercept him, but i take that opening to kick him in the back of the leg as hard as humanly possible. his injured calf causes his knee to buckle, and he drops to a crouch while gritting those gleaming fangs together.

Leech

the wolf is meaner than i gave him credit for. my skin has the consistency of hardened porcelain, but his fangs managed to puncture it. i'll make him pay for that. i'll lop off that shaggy head and nail it to the mantle of this blasted house before i'm through.

the wolf's human confederate makes another move, but i clip him under the jaw with an uppercut, and that sends him sprawling against one of the walls. his jaw should have shattered, but all it did was stun him. my suspicions are correct. the man has wolf blood in his veins, and the manifestation of this animal is connected to him.

i understand that if i slay just one of them, i'll be putting an end to them both. that suits me just fine. let them bleed together. i rise up and head over to the wolf, seeking to decapitate him first...but a rancid gurgling in my gut stops me.

there is a twisting pain lodged in the bottom of my abdomen, an anguish like serpents balling together inside of me and spewing out toxic venom. i wipe a hand across my mouth, and it is saturated in that black substance that came from the body of the host. it is not blood. it's something else, and it oh how it burns.

i tumble to the side and squeeze my arms as tightly as possible across my stomach. a stream of stinking vomit splatters from behind my fangs, and i go down to my hands and knees in the mess.

it is poison. this house has royally fucked me...

Wolf

the wolf is about to leap on the leech and finish him off, but i lift a hand to stop him. strangely enough, he complies. i don't want him getting a mouthful of whatever blistering poison it is that now has the vampyre writhing on the marble floor.

my hand lowers, and i place it across the wolf's head right between his ears. he does not shy away from my touch. he responds to it, pack member recognizing pack member. this moment doesn't last, because a deep rumbling comes from the bowels of the house. it rattles the entire structure, everything shaking and trembling in a violent upheaval.

the black wallpaper splits and contorts, and the fibers of the house seem almost to roar. another host emerges from the wall, the figure just detaching himself, pulling his tux from the surface and stepping out to meet us. he gestures broadly to a narrow hallway that has opened out of nowhere, several domed lights clattering and spinning with the movements of the house.

"the house has fed. it hunts and sniffs out prey much like your wolf. it dines on only the most irredeemable monsters. its belly is full now, and it will be moving on to a new hunting ground."

"the bond has been fulfilled. the connection is made, and your two halves are at peace. the wolf is tamed, and he'll no longer rampage without thought. you will guide him. the house has seen what lies in your heart, and the house finds you worthy. go now. go while it is still an option."

Leech

a toxin inside, and its corrosive, it boils and it burns and it makes me hate. i'd like nothing more than to chomp down on that wolf's cock and chew his drooping balls to gristle, but the animal is fleeing down a narrow hall with his human at his heels. i'm left to writhe, and the fetal position is a testament to wounded pride.

wounded, wounded, that's the theme. i gurgle, black slime oozing down the chin, and as the splatter of sick comes i take in a new angle of this execution room. the wallpaper is bending, tearing, shaping itself into more of those vexing hosts. from cratered wall-holes moths of yellow and black fly, big clumsy things, deathheads to herald death. the hosts are coming in hordes, cockroaches skittering for me, and soon i'm blinded by tuxedos, and limp hands lacking life start to peel at me and pull me in the direction of the wall and its metamorphosis.

they're soundless, these servants of the house, and i think of them as nothing more than drones in a hive, and it's the hivemind that wants me. is the house feminine? i think so. she's been a queen bitch so far, and i think she's more of a glutton than i've ever been. this can't be my fate. i'm destined to be…just food?!? i haven't felt this much pain since i was alive, and if the queen can hurt a corpse, then quite the queen she must be.

i go kicking, screaming, and biting. chunks of tux swirl around me, an undead twister intent on fucking up all that would seek to fuck me up.

the wallpaper has become a maw, and how fitting…that fangs await in the end…

Wolf

the house is shimmering, shaking, a volatile force, some starving engine that has finally located fuel. the smells blast us, floral, aphrodisiacs, siren scents of desire belching up from the underbelly of this sentient structure. is the house a plant? some malformed and gargantuan growth spat out from the rock of another world, long lost cousin to the venus flytrap, seeking to ensnare only the worst of us.

*i'll never know, and it's not important. what matters is that looming exit, the front door clapping open and closed like a tongue performing parlor tricks in a bar, and i don't intend to be the cherry stem that gets twisted up in the process. the wolf runs alongside me, just as stressed and seeking escapism. clouds of smoke kiss at our fleeing heels, the cigarette smog of monsters come and gone, dead or half-dead things that the house has consumed in **her** time.*

that pronoun seems to have come from nowhere. why do i suddenly think of the house as a her? a mad woman, a mother driven to desperation, the hosts her dutiful children all helping her to feed. forget it. the door is open, and we leap.

as soon as we make that leap, a schism inverts, and i feel the animal at my side meshing into me like a glob of paint. it's a marriage of fur and skin, wild and domesticated, man and wolf… he's coming back into me, and i suppose i'm going back into him. i don't fight it. i'm past that.

we're meant for each other.

Wolf

we're ejected out into the sagebrush, dusty and coughing, but whole. i flip onto my back, crab-walking across the ground in order to put distance between myself and the house that is not a house at all.

have you ever witnessed a human being suffering through a seizure? this is what seems to be happening to the house, but instead of limbs contorting violently, walls, doors, columns, and miscellaneous chunks of wood transform before my eyes. a predator shedding camouflage. doors swing outward like mouths sucking air, and great deathhead moths pour out with each exhale, flapping skyward in lazy flocks, their wing patterns tiny skulls dressed in tuxes.

the foundation levitates, a spinning ruin, and from the underside twelve stork-like legs sprout, a carapace seeming to shimmer into existence over certain exposed parts of the house. the legs move with the nimble gait of a spider on the hunt, and to my astonishment, the house walks in the direction of the horizon, the girth of it swaying back and forth, boards falling, nails shedding, doors breaking free of hinges to send mini-cataclysms across the dirt.

a single stained glass window looks back at me like an infected eye, red and smeared, a window that was never there before. a feral face rushes that window from inside, and i see it is the leech, battering his fists against glass that isn't glass, baring his teeth in a mixture of rage and lament. he is dragged back by host after host, and then his face is gone forever.

Wolf

the immensity of what i'm seeing has frozen me
in place. the house walks on the legs she grew,
the legs she hid in the soil, and her shambling
thorax sprouts wings, hideous wings of window
and piping, and she turns a bulbous head in my
direction over a shoulder of cellar, her mouth
opens, and her teeth are brass knobs, her eyes
are fireplaces still burning, and a bellow
comes from her shrapnel-lips, a lonely and
mournful sound, a foghorn that shakes the
ground, vibrates in the marrow of my bones.

there seems to be no real evil in her. a judge,
a jury, an executioner all in one, but only
because that is what some multi-dimensional
form of nature made her. just like me, she's
trying to survive in a world that is sometimes
cold and inhospitable. there's a lesson in her
hunger. she teaches with her wooden teeth.

i've learned not to fight what i am anymore.
she made me confront a part of myself that i
never liked, never wanted, and in the heart of
the house, i found clarity. i can't change the
wolf and he can't change me, but we can
compromise. we can live together as one, soul
of soul, and i think that's enough. i feel him
inside me now, smiling with canine teeth, and
the acceptance in those yellow eyes makes me
feel good, strong, and ready for the next
adventure. sometimes when you see the beast,
touch the beast, and listen to a heartbeat that
sounds much like your own…

you see how similar you really are. halves of a
whole. life, however different from your own,
is still life. i'm choosing life. i embrace it,
and i never thought it would be this warm.

the house lets her wings unfurl, and she takes to the sky, fumbling against the wind at first, an old dragon that has forgotten how to fly, but soon she finds her stride, and she's soaring, bits and pieces of foundation falling back to the earth, little souvenirs of her passing.

the migration begins anew, and this hunting ground has been played out. where she'll go now, i don't know. but the world has no shortage of monsters. the supernatural kind, and the human kind too. i hear the beating of her heart somewhere far above me like the distant drone of a boeing 747 in flight.

soon she is just a black speck in the clouds, a pinprick indistinct, bound for new constellations. i watch her for as long as i can. i commit her wings and her visions to memory.

nothing now but a canvas of light blue sky.

and the flutter of remembered wings...

Afterword

Hearts of Monsters has been a long time coming. I started the novella in 2016, and it has been cobbled together sporadically during a three year period, culminating in its ending in February of 2019. It's a story about personal growth, facing down the demons inside, and choosing to either conquer your sins or let them consume you.

I think we all have a little monster in us, but what matters is the heart beating within, and the paths we choose.

Follow your heart, even if it's a little dark and thorny, because it can lead you to wonderful places.

* — JM*

ABOUT THE AUTHOR:

When I was still a child and picked up my very first Goosebumps book by R. L. Stine, I knew I'd fallen head over heels in love with all things horror. It's a love affair that has only grown stronger over the years, a borderline obsession with stories that explore the darkest recesses of the human imagination. I guess you could say I'm like Thorny Rose in that way...always stalking down those special stories that have the ability to invoke a creepy-crawly feeling right down in the marrow of my bones.

As I grew older I discovered the work of some of my biggest inspirations like Stephen King, Edgar Allan Poe, H.P. Lovecraft, Clive Barker...and the work of those authors sent me deeper down the path of the macabre. During my teenage years I had the little tradition of reading Stephen King's The Stand each summer to lose myself in the devastation of the superflu and marvel at the sadistic magnetism of Randall Flagg.

I've devoured horror fiction for as long as I can remember and reading the words weaved by the greats of the genre inspired me to begin writing. I wanted the opportunity to tell my own tales with the intent to terrify, to disturb; to capture the morbid curiosity of the reader just as my own was caught so early on in life.

If I've managed to inspire some of those feelings in you, my readers, then I feel that I've accomplished something just a little bit magical. There's still some magic left in this world, and I think it's most powerful when manifested in the form of words scrawled across many blank pages. Granted any magic contained within my work will be of the dark variety...but I wouldn't want it any other way. ;)

Jeremy Megargee lives in Martinsburg, West Virginia. When he's not writing, he enjoys hiking mountain trails, weight training, getting tattooed and being a garden variety introvert. Oh, and reading too (duh).

Megargee is also the author of DIRT LULLABIES, SWEET TREATS, and OLD HOLLOW.

Connect with me online:

Facebook: www.facebook.com/JMHorrorFiction

Instagram: @xbadmoonrising

JM

Thanks for reading!

What did you think of HEARTS OF MONSTERS?

Feedback is incredibly important for indie authors. Most indie authors are not affiliated with Big Publishing and we don't have the vast resources or marketing tools to get our names out there compared to many of the advertised best-selling titles. Reviews give my work additional exposure and help new readers to discover my particular brand of horror.

If you enjoyed this book, I would love it if you could head over to the Amazon.com page for Hearts of Monsters and leave an honest review about what you thought of the story. I read every single review I get and I'm very grateful for the support.

Feel free to share this book with friends, word of mouth advertising goes a long way...and it helps the horror spread. ;)

Made in the USA
Middletown, DE
28 February 2022